"You don't l
means to m

"You're good peo

For some reason, his words of est her cheeks warm. "I love children…and babies. I'm happy to help you out."

"Great. Let's talk money."

"You don't even have to pay me if you'd do me a favor."

Joel faced her, his eyes wary. "What's the favor?"

Resisting the urge to squirm, Sienna cleared her throat. "I have three weddings to attend and I'd like you to be my date. A buffer between me and the eligible men."

Joel fidgeted. "I want your help with Micah but I don't know if this is such a good idea. This is a small town and everyone knows we can't stand each other."

"It would be a win-win for the both of us. I'm not looking for anyone and you would have someone to watch Micah anytime."

"You raise a good point." He mulled over her words and then tapped the wheel. "I'd be happy to be your pretend boo."

Zoey Marie Jackson loves writing sweet romances. She is almost never without a book and reads across genres. Originally from Jamaica, West Indies, she has earned degrees from New York University; State University of New York at Stony Brook; Teachers College, Columbia University; and Argosy University. She's been an educator for over twenty years. Zoey loves interacting with her readers. You can connect with her at zoeymariejackson.com.

Books by Zoey Marie Jackson

Love Inspired

The Adoption Surprise
The Christmas Switch

Visit the Author Profile page at LoveInspired.com.

Mother for a Month

Zoey Marie Jackson

ISBN-13: 978-1-335-58570-7

Mother for a Month

For questions and comments about the quality of this book, please contact us at CustomerService@Harlequin.com.

Love Inspired
22 Adelaide St. West, 41st Floor
Toronto, Ontario M5H 4E3, Canada
www.LoveInspired.com

Printed in U.S.A.

I will lift up mine eyes unto the hills, from whence cometh my help. My help cometh from the Lord, which made heaven and earth.

—*Psalm* 121:1–2

I would like to dedicate this book to my daughter-in-love, Jasmine Olivia. She is a new mother and watching her care for my first grandchild has been a blessing. She has been a gift to my son and it warms my heart watching them interact with each other as best friends while caring for their baby girl.

Thank you to my sister, who tears through my book in hours, a motivator for me to keep writing. Thank you to the wonderful Harlequin team and Melissa and my wonderful agent, Latoya. And finally, to my husband, my biggest supporter, talk-through partner and friend, I love you and appreciate your giving me the push to keep going.

Chapter One

Of all the locations in all the world, Joel Armstrong had to end up here—in Shreveport, Louisiana—on a Friday afternoon in this tiny blip of an airport. Sienna King leaned forward so her knotless auburn braids would cover her face while she read through her dissertation research on her iPad mini titled *The Effect Size of Teaching on Student Progress Despite Poverty and Parenting.* This was her fourth time reading through it after the humiliating faux pas during her defense the week before. But Sienna would have a second chance to present during the summer, and she was going to ensure there wouldn't be a need for a third.

Maybe Joel wouldn't spot her. Although, at five foot ten, she was hard to miss, especially with so many empty seats in the small waiting area. Still, a girl could hope.

A shadow loomed. In her peripheral view, Sienna saw a long, lanky frame slink into the seat next to her and gave him the side-eye. At six-four, Joel was one of the few men who truly towered over her. He had olive-toned skin like she did, a light beard and curls the girls seemed to love. He'd only recently started sporting a beard, which suited him.

"What are you doing here?" she asked, moving her braids off her face, not even trying to feign surprise or hide her irritation at her companion. This was how she communicated with Joel.

Ever since he had beaten her at the annual spelling bee in second grade—her parents had been mad at her for spelling the word *fuchsia* incorrectly—Sienna had been angry at Joel. He had preened over that plastic medal, keeping it on his desk just to taunt her, which lead to the birth of their decades-long rivalry. All through school, if she answered a question, he had the opposite response. The worst of it was in high school, when he received a perfect score on the SATs. Eventually, their interactions with each other became a habit. It was one she never intended to break.

Right as she asked the question, Sienna noticed he was holding a small, squirming bundle in his arms. "What is that?" She pointed; her eyes wide.

"What does it look like?" he shot back, lifting the baby boy to his shoulder and giving him an awkward pat on his back. At least, she presumed he was a boy, judging by the blue blanket dotted with gray elephants and baby bag. Suddenly, the baby opened his mouth, fully intending to suck on Joel's jacket. A very dirty jacket.

Sienna considered moving to another seat, but she couldn't risk the baby sucking on germs. She dropped her iPad in her bag and snatched—er, *rescued*—the infant from his clueless caretaker just as he stuck out his little tongue.

"What did you do that for?" Joel snapped, holding

on to the infant's legs with one hand while lifting his baseball cap to glare at her.

"What's the point of having a receiving blanket if you're not going to use it properly?" She jutted her chin toward him. "He was about to eat your filthy jacket. Although I'm not sure why you're wearing one in the month of June." Sienna made a show of placing the receiving blanket over her shirt and then cuddling the baby in her arms.

Releasing his hold, Joel rested his head against the wall. "Good catch. I didn't even think about it." He sighed. "Not even an hour, and I'm already failing at this whole babysitting thing. I don't know what made me say yes," he mumbled.

The baby fussed. "Where's his bottle?" she asked.

Joel fumbled around in the diaper bag and took out a small bottle.

Sienna popped it into the infant's mouth. He started sucking hard. "He is going at it," she observed, smiling at the bronzed face peering up at her.

"I couldn't get him to feed on the ride here," Joel breathed out, wiping his forehead.

When he was finished, the little one cooed. *Aw.* The sound went right into her heart. Sienna placed the bottle in the pocket of the diaper bag and held the baby to burp him. She closed her eyes, loving the feel of his cheek against her face—and that smell. The mixture of baby's breath, formula and newborn rolled into one intoxicating scent, making her ovaries scream. She patted his back, and he released a huge burp.

Chuckling, she asked Joel, "What's his name?"

Joel stretched and rested his hands on his jeans.

"Micah. He's my nephew." His brows furrowed. "My brother, Greg, and his wife, Tessa, live here in Shreveport. She had a medical emergency and is in the hospital, so Greg asked me to take care of Micah for a little while. He said it should only be a few weeks, tops."

"Your brother must have been really desperate to trust you with his newborn."

"More like overwhelmed. Micah is a little over three weeks old, and Greg has been toggling between caring for him and Tessa. Thankfully, he knows a judge and was able to get me temporary custody and Micah's birth certificate early."

Seeing the worry in Joel's dark brown eyes pricked her heart. "Sorry to hear that." She struggled to maintain a noncommittal tone, pressing her lips together to keep her curiosity sealed. Getting into other people's business meant you were inviting them into yours. And she sure didn't want Joel in hers. The very nature of his job as the town's reporter made him nosy. A nuisance. If there was something to know, Joel was the one to find out.

More passengers trickled over to the gate, sitting in the row ahead. Scanning the room, Sienna hoped there wouldn't be too many more.

"What brings you to Shreveport?" Joel inquired.

She adjusted the baby tummy-up on her lap. "A former student of mine is in the air force and invited me to his pinning ceremony as he was ranking up."

"Oh, that's right. There's a base about twenty minutes from here." He cocked his head. "That was nice of you to attend."

"He doesn't have any family, so I kept in touch with him through the years."

"And that's why you are Swallow's Creek's Teacher of the Year for two years in a row. I wish you would let me feature you in the town paper."

"I don't need recognition," she said, her tone frosty. "Whatever I do for others, it's because I care."

"All the more reason to let me do the story."

Joel had been pressing her to do the article since last year. She turned him down every time, but that didn't stop him from trying.

"See, this is why I don't try to have a conversation with you. You don't quit." Sienna pulled out a changing pad and a diaper, then changed Micah. Micah pumped his little legs. "Where's his car seat and stroller?" she asked once she was finished.

"I checked the car seat and didn't take the stroller," Joel said, pointing to the baby carrier on his chest. "I wanted to pack light. I'll buy whatever he needs once I'm home."

She snorted. "That was a big mistake. You're going to need a ton of stuff. These little guys come with a lot of baggage. You'll have to get a bassinet, formula, diapers…a baby cam. All of that."

"Yeah, I am clueless." He rubbed his chin and studied her. "You seem to know a lot about babies. Would you mind coming with me to the department store once we're back in town?"

"Ah… I don't know if I'm the right person for the job," she hedged, returning the baby to Joel. She grimaced at Joel's awkward attempts to hold the infant. "Maybe you could ask Jade or Kelsey," she said, referring to her best friends, who were mothers. Sienna was godmother to Jade's sixteen-year-old daughter, Izabella, and she played aunt to Kelsey's twin six-year-old stepdaughters, Mia and Morgan. Kelsey was also expecting and due sometime in early July.

"Thanks. I'll reach out..." He sounded lost. But Jade or Kelsey would set him straight, Sienna told herself, pushing back the small feeling of guilt. Micah chose that moment to release a little sigh, which tugged at her heart.

Kelsey's pregnancy had awakened Sienna's desire to be a mother, but until she was finished with her dissertation, everything else would have to wait, including motherhood. Sienna wanted to be a wife and then have children, and a husband wasn't on her must-have-anytime-soon list.

For now, her computer was her only serious relationship. That suited her just fine. Her laptop didn't fuss, didn't complain, and when she was tired of it, all she had to do was close the lid.

In the meantime, Sienna fed her maternal instincts by volunteering in the nursery at church. The head organizer was on vacation that week, and Sienna was the lead caretaker in her absence.

"Are you connecting in Dallas or Charlotte?" Joel asked.

"Dallas."

"So am I. Where are you sitting?"

She huffed. "On a seat inside the plane. Where do you expect me to be? On the wing?" She knew she was being snarky, but really, he just asked too many questions.

Joel held up a hand. "Just making conversation." Even though more passengers had trickled over to the gate, Sienna deduced their flight wouldn't be full, which was good news.

The flight crew walked up to the podium, and the attendant shared with the passengers that the plane was being cleaned and prepared for takeoff. Sienna glanced at her watch. Boarding would begin in about ten minutes. Joel excused himself, leaving the diaper bag with her, and strolled up to the counter.

Sienna decided to text her *Three Amigas* group, which consisted of herself, Kelsey and Jade. Her fingers glided across the screen. Guess who I ran into?

Your future husband, Jade shot back. Sienna sent a gagging emoji.

I wish, she replied.

Jade sent three question marks.

Joel's here and get this. He's coming back to DE with a baby.

Kelsey's answer was instant. Hold up. Joel's got a baby mama?

No. His nephew. Sienna looked up and saw Joel heading back her way. The attendant announced they were going to be boarding soon. Gotta go. Talk later. She slipped the phone into her purse.

Joel returned and asked, "What zone are you in?"

"I'm zone six," Sienna said.

"If you want, I can upgrade our tickets to first class. I could use help with the baby, and I'm too tall to be cramped on that small plane. I need all the leg room I can get."

How can he afford an upgrade? she wondered. He was a small-town reporter. But it wasn't her business.

He tapped his feet. "Well? Do you want it or not?"

Her instinct was to decline, but the baby shouldn't have to endure the plane ride with an amateur. Besides, Sienna couldn't resist being better than Joel, and helping with Micah would be a good way to rub it in his face. She smirked. "When you put it like that, how can I say no?"

"You could just say thank you." He grabbed his backpack and diaper bag, then marched up to the counter. She stood, gathered her belongings and accompanied Joel to get the new ticket. Sienna mumbled her appreciation. She knew she should be gracious, but being in Joel's presence made her cranky. Within minutes, they were settled together in the airplane with the baby nestled on his lap, fast asleep.

At one point of their journey, an older woman across the aisle looked over at them and smiled. "Such a good baby. You guys make a beautiful family."

Since he was in the aisle seat, Joel thanked the woman, which led to her chattering on about her own grandchildren. However, Sienna remained silent, sucker punched by the woman's assumption that she was Micah's mother. She stole a glance at Micah. How she wished she could claim this adorable child. She looked out the window, once again yearning to know how it would feel to bear life.

Her parents' mantra, *Education before love and marriage,* counteracted her biological clock. Her overachieving parents had hammered that into her since she was a child. By the end of the summer, she would finally be Dr. Sienna King, and she could erase the mental image of her parents' disappointed faces during her dissertation defense out of her mind.

Two days later, Joel stood before her outside the children's nursery at Millennial House of Praise, begging Sienna for assistance. If it had been anyone other than him, Sienna would have said yes; that's what he believed. But Sienna had dubbed him the most annoying man in Swallow's Creek. For the past twenty-four years, she had treated him like a gnat, an irritant, and for the most part, Joel was fine with it. Except for now. He needed her help.

Badly.

Joel raked his fingers through his locks. He needed a haircut, a shave…and some sleep. None of which he could do because of an eight-pound invasion in his life. His nephew had spent almost all of the past forty-eight hours crying. Micah cried until his voice was hoarse, but Joel couldn't get him to eat. Not that Joel had told his brother any of that. For Greg, Joel had been upbeat, assuring him that he had everything under control.

This morning, he woke up realizing he needed to be in church for two reasons: his brother needed prayers, and the church had a nursery. Free day care. Joel had gotten himself and Micah dressed in under thirty minutes and rushed through the door. He figured someone there could refer him to a nanny. There were three child-care centers in town and all were at capacity, including the two in-home day cares that he had called. He needed to find someone to care for his nephew while he worked. Fast.

He hadn't expected to bump into the full-figured beauty inside the nursery. For a moment, it irked him that they seemed to be in each other's faces of late.

Actually… Sienna might be the ideal person to ask to watch Micah. She had already bonded with him, plus school was out and she wasn't running the church's summer camp this year. Joel wasn't a member of the church, but he knew the church was renovating this summer. The more he thought about it, the more the idea held appeal.

He rubbed the bridge of his nose and decided to ask. "Would you be interested in watching Micah for me?"

Sienna ran her long nails—blinged-out with gems and pink tips—through her long braids. "Isn't there anyone else you can ask?" she whispered, mindful of the four sleeping babies in her charge, one of whom was Micah. She gestured for Joel to meet her outside so they could talk.

As soon as they were in the hallway, Joel continued. "I wouldn't ask if I weren't desperate. I can tell Micah likes you, and you were amazing with him during the plane ride." It took a lot for Joel to confess that Sienna was better than him at something.

Micah had fussed for a good portion of the second flight and was resting his head on Sienna's chest while she hummed a tune Joel didn't recognize. It was the only thing that soothed him. If not for her, Joel was certain he wouldn't have survived the journey home.

She lifted her chin and bragged, "That's because Micah knows I'm good people. I've heard that babies can sense the true nature of those around them."

He clenched his teeth. "That's ridiculous. He likes me as well. I'm sure I'll get the hang of it soon enough."

"Well, then you don't need me." She started to turn away, but he touched her arm.

He warned his wayward tongue that now wasn't the time for a verbal sparring and backtracked. "I didn't mean that. You're way better with Micah than I am. For now." He wiped his brow with the back of his hand and forced a smile on his face.

"Watching him for a few hours isn't the same as watching him all day." Her deep dimples appeared as she emphasized her point.

He tried to hold on to his patience. "You'd be helping out a friend." Joel knew Sienna hated when he teased her by calling her his friend.

She bristled. "Please. Don't get it twisted. You and I are nowhere near being friends. I *tolerate* you. There's a difference."

"We've known each other for over two decades. We're practically family."

Sienna pulled her orange cardigan close to her chest. "I can't with you."

"It's a paid gig," he said. Sienna was feisty, but she was also one of the most caring individuals he knew to everyone but him. Maybe it was time he explained everything. Maybe then she would help. "My boss, Skip, is retiring in a year, and I've just been promoted to associate editor at the newspaper. The plan is for me to move into his position—which is a massive accomplishment at only thirty-one—so I'll be taking on more tasks. There's no way I'm going to be able to juggle my schedule and take care of Micah. My brother's wife is in critical condition, and I can't have Micah neglected." He clasped his hands. "I'm not too proud to admit I'm overwhelmed."

"You mean to tell me that there's something Mr. Perfect SAT can't do?"

His left eye ticked. "I wish you'd stop bringing that up. It's a score. A fluke."

"Of course you'd say that. Some of us had to pull all-nighters to get a good score."

"Let's not get offtrack." Joel then asked, "Will you watch Micah for me? It's only for a few weeks."

Sienna's brown eyes softened. "I didn't get all that education to be a glorified nanny." She smoothed out her striped dress.

Her tone indicated that she was on the verge of relenting. Joel drew close. "Picture Micah's little face. You can't leave him in the hands of his unskilled uncle. He won't survive." He wiped his hands on his slacks, his heart pounding while he waited for her response.

"You don't play fair." Then her lips quirked. "The little guy is adorable. I've got to admit, he's hard to resist. I'll think about it. That's the best I can do." She touched his arm briefly. "Did you get his stuff yet?"

"Neither Kelsey nor Jade were available to help me. But if you give me a list, I'll go get everything after the service." He could hear the praise music starting up in the sanctuary. A few parishioners walked by, and he gave them a wave, ignoring their curious stares.

She appeared to wrestle with herself before she emitted a huge sigh. "Fine. I'll go with you. Meet me at my apartment, and we'll go get everything he needs. Do you know where I live?"

The fear around his chest calmed. "Thank you. Thank you. And, yes, I do know where to find you."

"Just so we're clear, if I did take the nanny gig, I'd be doing it for Micah. Not you."

He chuckled. "Fair enough. I'll be Micah's mouth-piece and utter a big thank-you for even thinking about it." He moved to give her a hug just to annoy her, but Sienna brushed him off.

"Keep your distance. I'm saving all my hugs for Micah."

With a laugh, Joel gave her a thumbs-up and walked toward the sanctuary, his steps light. For the first time since his brother had reached out for his help, Joel felt hopeful. One thing he knew about Sienna was that she did nothing by half measures; he was sure his wallet would see proof of that later. But Joel had no problem parting with his funds—that, he could handle. Money was uncomplicated. Taking care of Micah's emotional needs was what terrified him. But Sienna's presence could take care of that. Between his money and her heart, Micah would be fine. He just needed her to com-mit.

Chapter Two

"These people are taking the whole *a June bride is a bride for life* thing way too serious," Sienna mumbled. She had just gotten in from church and changed into a pair of white jeans, a pink T-shirt and her pink-and-white Chuck Taylors when she decided to check her calendar. She had not one, not two, but three weddings to attend this summer, and the first was a little over a week away. She groaned.

Kelsey was battling morning sickness, and Jade hadn't been invited, so Sienna would be going solo. *Ugh.* She didn't relish getting hit on because the men would think she was lonely without a plus one.

Her stomach grumbled, so she made her way into the kitchen of her two-bedroom apartment, which had been decorated with a checkered theme. Sienna had added green accents to brighten the room. She raised the blinds to let sunlight inside and opened her refrigerator to see almost-bare shelves. She needed to go grocery shopping. Next, Sienna searched her pantry for her cheese crackers. Then she remembered she had tossed her expired snacks before going to Shreveport. She snapped her fingers. She had bought an apple at the airport that she hadn't eaten.

After digging the apple out of her travel bag, she washed it, took a bite and checked her cell phone. Joel had texted that he was on his way. Her stomach quivered at the thought of seeing the little munchkin again. She wouldn't admit it, but she had held Micah a little longer than necessary in the church nursery. Maybe it was because his mother was far away in a hospital, but she'd bonded with him instantaneously. His little finger curling around hers had warmed her heart.

Watching Micah wouldn't be an inconvenience. In fact, it would give her a real dose of motherhood. Would it be enough to cure her? Or would it leave her craving more? She drew in a breath. There was only one way to find out.

Her cell phone vibrated, and she checked the screen. Seeing it was her mother on FaceTime, Sienna prayed for patience. She tapped Accept. "Before you say anything, I've been studying around the clock, Mom. I'm sure I'll pass the defense next time."

Her mother, Daphne, frowned. "You shouldn't have had to do a second defense. But that's not why I called."

Sienna squinted, wrinkling her nose. "Are you okay?" Her mother's brown skin was beaded with sweat, and she seemed out of breath. Sienna was her mini-me in every way, except Daphne was slender and Sienna was full-figured. Her mother never made Sienna's weight an issue—but in everything else, she was unrelenting.

Daphne waved a hand. "Yes. Don't try to change the

subject. Your father and I have found the perfect man for you. He's a surgeon and single."

"What about 'education before love'?" Sienna reminded her.

Daphne shrugged. "I think it's time for a new outlook. It would please us if you met him."

"Hmm… We'll see. I have to get going. I'll talk to you later, Mom." Sienna blew a kiss and ended the call. Her chest heaved. It was bad enough her parents tried to dictate her every move; now her mother was interfering in her love life. Her nonexistent-by-choice love life. Sienna wasn't having that. If she knew her parents, this was just the beginning. She had to find a way to thwart their intentions, or she would cave. Try to please them, even though experience had shown her countless times that was impossible. She should have just said she was already dating someone. That would've put a stop to it.

After finishing her apple, Sienna tossed the remnants in the trash and washed her hands. Her cell phone chimed; Joel was in the parking lot. She grabbed her purse and made her way down the stairs. Since she hadn't been able to snag a first-floor apartment, she liked the convenience of being near the staircase by the parking lot. Before getting in Joel's shiny new Jeep, she opened the rear passenger door to look at Micah in his car seat. His head was tilted, and his big brown eyes were pinned on her. Even though he was a newborn, he had a lot of curls—part of his Native American heritage—like his uncle. Both Joel's parents had Black and Native American heritage, and those traits had passed on to both generations.

She touched the infant's legs— "Hey, Micah." Realizing Joel waited for her, she closed the door and got in the front the seat. She greeted Joel. He had changed into a pair of dark blue jeans and a blue T-shirt with the word *Shreveport* imprinted across the chest. Just then, her stomach growled. “Did you eat yet?”

He shook his head. “No. I didn’t want to keep you waiting.”

“I didn’t eat anything either. Can we hit up the drive-through?”

“Sure.” He exited the lot. “Where do you think you want to eat?”

“I can call and order pretzels and lemonades from Patty’s, and we can grab and go. How does that sound?”

“Perfect. Patty’s lemonades are the truth.” Joel turned toward the direction of Patty’s Pretzels. He hummed a praise tune under his breath that sounded like “Way Maker,” which was one of the songs the team had sung earlier in the service. His voice was low, but it sounded like he could hold a tune. For a second, Sienna was tempted to join in, but she held back. It wasn’t that kind of a party. She tapped her chin. But… Joel might be the perfect solution to quash her parents’ matchmaking attempts. Even as the thought came, she rejected it. Sienna didn’t know if she could do anything that put her in Joel’s presence on purpose, and her parents would want to meet him.

Squinting against the sun’s glare, she pulled down the visor before searching in her purse for her sunglasses. She made a mental note to get visors for the rear windows. “Have you heard from your brother?” she asked once she had called in their meals.

“Yes, he called last night. Tessa is in a coma. She

hemorrhaged, and that's why Greg had to rush her to the hospital. He said they had to do a transfusion."

She gasped, then touched Joel's arm. "I'm sorry to hear that." That bit of news helped her decide on Micah's care. "Well, the next time you speak to him, you let him know that his son is in good hands—mine. And I'll add her to my prayer list."

Joel looked over at her briefly before returning his attention to the road. "Thank you. Thank you. You don't know how much this means to me. You're good people, Sienna King."

For some reason, his words of esteem made her cheeks warm. "I'm happy to help your brother out during his time of need." She was surprised to find how much she meant it.

"Great. Let's talk money." As he pulled into the parking lot for Patty's Pretzels, he rattled off a number that made her brows rise to her forehead. Sienna directed him to park at the pick-up spot marked number three. One of the workers would bring out their food.

"Are you related to the Rockefellers or the Vanderbilts?"

"I minored in accounting and I've been investing my money since my teens. Without telling you my business, I have enough to retire right now if I choose. But I love my job, so..."

Figures. "I don't need that much money." Turning her head to check on Micah, Sienna relaxed when she saw he was asleep. She flicked dust off her white pants. "Actually, you don't even have to pay me if you'd do me a favor."

Putting the Jeep in Park, Joel faced her, his eyes wary. "What's the favor?"

Sienna gave a laugh that sounded more like a shriek. "You don't have to get suspicious." She tapped his arm. "So relax."

He leaned into his seat and pinned her with an intense gaze. "What do you need me to do?"

Resisting the urge to squirm, Sienna cleared her throat. "I have three weddings to attend, and I'd like you to be a buffer between me and the men who seem to think that because you're single, you must be desperate."

He lifted a brow. "We both know you can't stand me, though I've done nothing to you. Why would you want to spend so much time with me? Even though I'm probably invited as well."

"Because you're convenient," she rushed to explain. "And like you said, you're most likely on the guest list."

Joel shifted in his seat. "I want your help with Micah, but I don't know if this is such a good idea. This is a small town, and everyone knows we can't stand each other."

"It would be a win-win for the both of us. Weddings and funerals can be chief hookup events. I'm not looking for anyone, and you would have someone to watch Micah anytime since I know news doesn't just happen from nine to five."

"You raise a good point. I hadn't thought of that." He mulled over her words and then tapped the wheel. "I'd be happy to be your pretend boo."

"'Pretend boo'?" She giggled and shoved his arm, causing him to jerk from the impact. "You are so silly."

A young man headed their way with food bags, gesturing for Joel to roll down his window. Sienna started to retrieve her wallet, but Joel put up a hand to say he would pay. "I don't need you to pay for my food," she insisted.

"I don't mind paying."

By then, the youth was standing by the vehicle, waiting for payment.

Sienna huffed. "That's not the point."

Joel's voice rose, causing Micah to stir. "Must we argue about everything?"

Sienna hated knowing Micah was getting upset because of their fussing, so she backed down and allowed Joel to settle the tab. She bit into her pretzel and allowed several tense seconds to pass. Then she asked, "For Micah's sake, can we *try* to get along?"

"Can you not be so cantankerous? You bait me for no reason."

It was true. She drew in a breath. "I'll do better." She gave him a side glance and returned to their previous conversation. "So do we have a deal?"

Joel sounded doubtful. "I don't know, because all we do is bicker when we're within five feet of each other. No one is going to believe we're dating."

She gritted her teeth. "We can be civil. I know we can."

Joel chuckled, releasing the tension in the car. "If you say so." Then he held out a fist. "All right, I'm in. The way I see it, I'm getting a bargain. I accompany a beautiful woman to a few weddings in exchange for babysitting services. That's a no-brainer for me."

She lowered her lashes and joked, "I do have to agree." They shared a laugh. Sienna felt a pleasant sensation warm her insides, and she questioned why. He wasn't the first man to compliment her, but he was the first to make her feel like a schoolgirl again in a long time.

Pushing a dolly behind Sienna's cart—which carried Micah in his car seat and a few other items on her never-ending list—Joel made his way to the long checkout line. Within a minute or two of entering the baby section, Joel had known he was dealing with a retail professional. After Sienna had directed him to get a dolly, she then placed boxes containing a swing, bassinet, stroller, diapers, wipes, formula and bedding on top. Then she had added clothes, pacifiers, bottles, a bottle warmer and other stuff she declared essential.

Joel didn't understand how an infant needed so many things. Sienna had assured him that she would help him organize everything, which was a major relief.

The cashier's mouth dropped. "You guys waited until the last minute to shop for your baby, and now you're paying for it."

Sienna gave her an awkward laugh. "Yes, but our little Micah is well worth it."

"I hear you." The cashier proceeded to ring up their order.

She hadn't corrected the young lady's assumption about Micah's parentage, and Joel figured it was best he do the same. It would be too long of an explanation. Sienna had already suggested he donate the items to the women's shelter once Micah returned home to his parents.

As he watched Sienna place items on the conveyor belt, her request for him to be her wedding date came to mind. He wondered why she wasn't interested in dating and decided to ask her once they had left the store and packed everything into the Jeep.

"I have to focus on my dissertation," she said. "And relationships are a lot of work that I don't have time for right now—if ever." Then she turned the question back on him. "What about you? I take it you're not seeing anyone, or you wouldn't have consented to be my fake date."

"What does it matter?" he said, then remembered he needed her help, and tried to keep the agitation out of his voice. Something about her just always put him on edge. "Sorry about that. I… I'm not dating either. And, like you, I have no desire to date."

"Why not?" She wiggled her eyebrows. "You're one of Swallow's Creek's most eligible bachelors."

He gave her the side-eye, knowing she was referring to his exposé on Zachary Johnson, her best friend Kelsey's husband. "My boss made me do that. We sold a lot of papers that week." Zachary, a widower at the time, had moved to town the year before and had captured the attention of Swallow's Creek's single ladies.

"So back to my question. If you're not dating, it's because you don't want to?"

He shifted, uncomfortable with her question.

She chuckled. "I see you don't like being interrogated either."

Wiping a hand on his T-shirt, he said, "Like you, I'm busy with my career. Plus, I'm sure you heard my sad story from years ago." Closing the rear gate, the conversation came to a halt until he was close to his home.

"So, are you going to tell me the sad story?" Sienna asked, her brows furrowed.

He slid a glance her way to see if she was being genuine. There were no secrets in Swallow's Creek. She must have heard about his broken engagement, because it had been the subject of gossip for months. The fact that his fiancée had been of a different race seemed to only add fuel to the fire.

"There's no need to pretend you don't know about the disastrous fate of my relationship," he said, pulling into this driveway. "It's been about eight years. Believe me, I am over it—and her."

Her mouth dropped. "I'd forgotten about that. How did I not remember that you got jilted?" Then she added, "I think I was away at school when I heard about it, but I don't make it a point to keep track of your love life." Her jab wasn't lost on him.

He opened the door for her. "Well, I wasn't left at the altar. Long story short, I was engaged, and my parents didn't approve. Actually, my father didn't. He offered Elizabeth money to break things off with me, and she took it. She left me a month before we were supposed to walk down the aisle."

After pressing the button to open the rear gate, Joel grabbed the box with the bassinet and steeled himself for Sienna's smart remarks. To his surprise, she touched his arm. "I'm sorry that happened to you."

He stilled. Their eyes locked before she looked away and fiddled with her braids.

"You surprise me. I thought you would be gloating at my past humiliation."

"Wow. That stings." Her voice caught. "I suppose I

could see why you would think so, though." She lowered her chin. Joel wanted to touch her cheek and reassure her that it was okay. But rehashing his past had caused a surprising pang in his heart.

"Let's get Micah inside." He headed up his driveway to open the front door while Sienna popped the carrier out of the car seat. When she entered his home, she wouldn't meet his eyes.

Taking Micah out of the carrier, Sienna laid him down on the sofa and dug into the baby bag for a diaper. Joel didn't want things to be weird between them. "Sienna, I'm used to you snapping at me, and I'm just as quick with the comebacks. It's what we do, what we've always done. I just assumed that when you brought up the topic, it was more of the same." He pried open the box so he could set up the bassinet. Micah had slept with him in his king-size bed the last two days, and Joel had been afraid of rolling on top of him.

She shook her head. "I wouldn't make fun of something like that. What she did to you was horrible. Forgive me for saying this, but your father's actions were reprehensible too." Sienna's eyes flashed. "What kind of parent does that to their child?" Her tone mirrored the disgust he felt.

Joel took a step back. Sienna asked the question that had plagued him for months after the incident. It had driven a deep wedge between him and his parents because his mother had defended his father's actions. She hadn't agreed with his wanting to marry a white woman. His heart constricted when he thought about the almost nonexistent relationship he'd had with his mother right before his parents passed. In a low voice, he said, "Not everyone was meant to be a parent."

"I wish I didn't know firsthand that you spoke the truth," Sienna said, seemingly more to herself than him. Joel paused. It appeared as if they might have something in common. He wanted to delve into that but decided not to press her for details. Instead, he busied himself with getting the rest of the baby stuff out of his Jeep. He and Sienna then assembled Micah's room, decorating it with an elephant theme. Joel had chosen the smaller of the two bedrooms closest to the master bedroom.

Next, Sienna walked him through how to change Micah's diaper properly as well as how to prepare his formula. But in the back of his mind, Joel played back her softly spoken words. He and Sienna were natural adversaries. Joel had never once considered that they shared anything in common or that they could complete a task without arguing. Whenever he was in Sienna's presence, Joel steeled himself against the insults she would toss out, and he was always seeking a way out. But that evening, once they were done with Micah's room, they shared a pizza together and watched Micah sleep, and he regretted it when their time came to an end and Sienna went home.

How weird was that?

Chapter Three

"So let me see if I've got this right," Kelsey said, seated at the kitchen table in Joel's home. The table was a deep-espresso color, with a bench on one side and chairs on the other. "You are spending your much-needed summer vacation to be a nanny for Joel's nephew? Why didn't you refer him to someone else?"

"It's only for a month or so. I took the job because I like Micah. That sweet face is hard to resist." She pulled back instinctively when Kelsey reached over to touch her forehead. Her brows furrowed. "What are you doing?"

"I'm checking to see if you have a fever."

Jade laughed. "Does she? Because I never thought I'd see the day when Sienna talk about Joel without an ounce of animosity."

"He's not that bad..." Sienna trailed off, noting the shocked looks on her friends' faces. The three friends got together every other Sunday for fellowship and to catch up on their lives. They usually rotated at one another's houses, but Sienna had asked for their meeting this Sunday to be at Joel's house since she would be watching Micah.

She turned up the baby monitor. "Can you two be serious for one moment? We need to get our devotions finished before Micah wakes up." Joel had called Sienna early that morning to ask if she could watch Micah because he had a robbery turned arson at Mr. MacGrady's he had to cover for the paper.

Mr. MacGrady's was a local diner that had become a staple in their town; Sienna and her friends frequented there often. They even had their favorite booth. Sienna had rushed over in her pajamas and had gotten dressed in a plaid jumpsuit and cardigan in Joel's spare room. She didn't share that tidbit of information with her friends, though.

Jade shifted, causing her bright yellow earrings to sway. She was dressed in a yellow romper and had coordinated her jewelry perfectly. "Forgive us if our brains are too full with this juicy development to concentrate."

"Yeah. You'd better take the ribbing, because you were the chief instigator back when I was dating Zachary." Kelsey gave her a light jab. Sienna noted her friend's thin fingers, and her heart squeezed. Kelsey had been suffering from terrible morning sickness and had developed anemia. As a result, she wore a light sweater over her T-shirt and leggings to keep warm.

Sienna folded her arms. "Well, this is different. It was obvious that you and Zachary had chemistry. Joel and I can barely stand to be in each other's presence." A flash of them eating pizza and setting up Micah's room came to mind, disproving her words.

"Oh, but you seem to be adjusting just fine." Jade

waggled her eyebrows "After all, pretend dating is still dating."

"I predict Sienna and Joel are going to be at each other's throats before the end of the week," Kelsey said. "You can't be around each other without bickering."

Sienna couldn't hold back her laugh. "You two are a mess. Joel and I called a truce. We're mature enough to put aside our differences and focus on Micah." She drummed her fingers on the table. "We both want the best for Micah, and we're capable of behaving like the professionals we are."

Kelsey scoffed. "Huh. I'll believe when I see it."

"I have my own prediction. After a month, Joel and I will come out unscathed and without a single argument." On the inside, she gasped. Was her competitive nature the reason for that bold statement? Maybe she should amend it to something like, less than five arguments?

"Mark my words—you won't last a day. Make that an hour," Kelsey said with a pointed stare.

"Whatever. You'll see."

The women moved on with their devotions. Sienna asked for prayers for Joel's brother and sister-in-law, and of course, they prayed for Micah. Just as their prayers ended, Sienna's phone buzzed. Coming home for lunch. Can I grab you something? She smiled.

She replied, Sure. I'll take a turkey sandwich and a diet cola. Thanks. After she hit Send, Sienna looked up to see Jade's and Kelsey's mouths hanging open. "What?" She rolled her eyes. "Don't go reading anything into that."

"You two seem so…domesticated," Kelsey taunted.

Sienna rolled her eyes again, then shifted the conversation. "Watching Micah will be a welcome respite while I revise my dissertation. I plan to work on it during the times when he's sleeping."

"Take it easy on yourself." Jade's eyes held sympathy. Sienna knew her friend was thinking about her blunder during her dissertation defense.

But she couldn't. She couldn't *take it easy* when that error had been the biggest of her life. Just thinking about how she had gone blank and spewed incorrect facts made Sienna squirm with shame. She nodded, unable to meet Jade's sympathetic eyes. She hated that she'd messed up. Failed. Her mortification had been magnified by her parents' presence. She could still see their stern faces. If it weren't for Kelsey and Jade, Sienna didn't know how she would have finished her last days at work. Unbeknownst to Sienna at the time, her principal and team had planned a huge celebration. Her friends had made sure to alert her coworkers, even showing up at her school the next day to have lunch with her in her classroom, just to check on her.

"You've got this," Kelsey cheered before slapping a hand over her mouth and rushing to the bathroom.

Both she and Jade rushed to help Kelsey. Jade placed a cool cloth on Kelsey's forehead, and Sienna made some tea. She had just finished pouring Kelsey a cup when Joel popped in through the door. He was covered in soot from head to toe.

He felt the heat of three pairs of eyes. Joel shifted uncomfortably, knowing he looked worse than he felt. Whoever had robbed Mr. MacGrady's had also set fire to the bathroom, and Joel had volunteered to help with the cleanup. He wasn't used to coming home to anyone and hadn't considered the picture he presented when he walked through the door.

Sienna wrinkled her nose. "You look terrible. Why did you come through the front door? You should have entered through the garage."

"I…uh…" Joel took a step back, their lunch hanging from his hand. He looked around in disbelief. Jade's eyes were popped wide open. Kelsey coughed, covering her mouth, but he could see her lips twitch. Then he addressed the sassiest of the women. "Last I checked, the deed was in my name only." He expected her to back off or apologize, but this was Sienna.

Raising her brows, she snapped back, "And last I checked, you have a newborn in this house who doesn't have all his shots yet." Then she shooed him outside. Yes—*shooed him* like he was a nuisance. The gall.

This time, her friends couldn't hide their mirth, especially when, for some reason, Sienna flashed them a glance, "This isn't an argument. It's common sense."

Joel's left eye ticked at the *common sense* jab. It wasn't like he was a real father. Micah had been in his care for less than a week. Nevertheless, he clamped his jaw and stomped outside, fuming. He was tired and hungry and wanted to eat, shower and catch a nap. The garage door cracked open, and Jade stood in the doorway.

"Her delivery could use some polish," Jade said, taking the bag from him. "But you know she means well."

Joel gave a quick nod and went into the half bath to wash his face and hands. When he saw his reflection, he drew in a harsh breath. He was filthy. Even his beard was covered with soot. His anger subsided, and he acknowledged that Sienna was right. He hadn't been thinking about his nephew's welfare when he barged into the house. Joel darted upstairs to clean up and change his clothes. Then he approached Sienna and apologized. "You were right."

He saw Kelsey and Jade eye each other with disbelief but kept his attention on Sienna.

With a quick nod, Sienna sniffed. "I'm sorry if I sound harsh, but I'm trying to care for the little guy."

"I know you are," Joel said.

She gestured to the table, where she had placed his lunch on a plate. Joel had ordered a Mexican rice bowl and salad. He slipped into the chair. Sienna made sure to remind him to bless his meal before eating. Her friends must have seen that as their cue to leave. The women hugged like they weren't going to see each other again, though he knew they planned to get together in a couple of days for a movie night. He caught Kelsey and Jade giving Sienna warning glares before waving at him and going through the door.

Micah's fiery defender looked penitent and unsure. She sat across from him, her head lowered. "While you were washing up, my friends pointed out that I was out of line." Joel nodded as he took a sip of juice. Then she said, "I want to apologize for embarrassing you in front of Kelsey and Jade."

He almost choked and began coughing on reflex. But he accepted her apology—especially since she seemed so sincere. Although this was so unlike the Sienna he knew. "I've known them as long as you have. It's all good. I have thick skin," he said.

"Great. We're fully capable of being civil and communicating with decency." She bit into her sandwich.

Joel chewed slowly. He had no idea how to react when she was behaving so oddly. "Who are you trying to convince?" he asked. "Me or you?"

"What I'm trying to say here is that I'm going to be more respectful," she snapped. "Why can't you accept that instead of..." She stopped and drew in a few deep breaths. Then she took another bite of her sandwich, chewing and thinking.

"Just be you," Joel said. "I like you just fine the way you are."

Her lips quirked. This time she met his gaze with a challenging one of her own. "So you don't think my mouth is like a razor?"

"Oh, I do. It's sharp. But I prefer knowing how you feel upfront than having you gloss over your feelings with a fake smile."

She released a sigh. "I'm so glad you said that, because biting my tongue around you would be hard work."

He cracked up. "Good. Now you don't have to. Besides, I'm going to need your humor when we attend these weddings together."

Just then, Micah cried out, and Sienna rushed over to tend to him. Joel watched her move, concern etched across her face, and smiled. One thing he could say about Sienna was that spending time with her would never be dull. And though he would never admit it, being in her presence gave him a zing. A zest he didn't know he had been missing.

Chapter Four

The Three Amigas gathered at Jade's house for dinner and a movie. It had been a few weeks since they had gotten together for a movie night, which was unusual for them, but their lives had gotten hectic over the past year. Kelsey was often busy with her twin daughters and with the effects of her pregnancy. Fortunately, Kelsey was in her final trimester and was looking forward to welcoming her son in a couple months. Jade was preoccupied with opening her personal gym, and Sienna had been focused on completing her dissertation.

"What's going on in that head of yours?" Jade asked Kelsey while whipping mashed potatoes. Jade's kitchen was a cook's dream, with lots of counter space, storage and top-level appliances. She had completed most of the work—like the backsplash and floors—herself by watching YouTube videos. Jade had two whole baked chickens and brussels sprouts roasting in the oven because that was Jade. No popcorn or candy for movie night.

The smells made Sienna's stomach growl loud enough

that she feared it would wake Micah. Sienna had bundled up the infant to take him with her since Joel was working late. Micah was now asleep in his bassinet next to her on the couch. She watched him while he slumbered, and her desire for motherhood intensified.

"What are the odds that Sienna and Joel would both be on the same plane at the same time all the way in Louisiana?" Kelsey pointed at Sienna. "Now look at her. She can't keep her eyes off him. Makes you wonder if it's the same with Joel." She popped a grape into her mouth, her wedding ring twinkling under the lights. Kelsey was about to celebrate her one-year anniversary in the fall.

"Really? That's what you're thinking about?" Sienna rolled her eyes. "Listen, just because you married your crush, that don't mean the rest of us are in a hurry to get hitched. I told you already that my computer is all the company I need, besides you guys and God."

"I think she's protesting too much," Jade said with a chuckle.

"I agree." Kelsey said, finishing her last grape. She rubbed her tummy. "Joel is eye candy. He's like Clark Kent hiding under that cap."

She knew they were teasing her because they thought Sienna was easy to bait. "I prefer chocolate over candy. And Joel and I are just… Well, we've reached an understanding."

"Oh, that's what they call it these days? An *understanding*?" Jade retrieved plates and utensils out of the cupboard and rested them on the counter. "You've got to forgive me. I've been out of the dating loop too long."

Kelsey snickered.

"Whatever. I can't with you two. Quit messing with me and put on the movie."

The friends all wanted to watch a movie about a single mother of three boys who baked cakes in order to save her home. Jade had it pulled up and frozen on the screen.

"Guess what time it is," Jade singsonged. She scooped the mashed potatoes into a bowl and then bent over to take the chickens out of the oven.

"Time for some good eats." Sienna eyed the food. "My mouth is watering with anticipation right now."

"Get the tray tables," Jade ordered. "We can each serve ourselves and chow down while we're watching."

Sienna fixed Kelsey a small serving of mashed potatoes before helping herself. Jade poured freshly made iced tea.

"Mmm… These mashed potatoes are giving me life right now," Kelsey said, closing her eyes. "So creamy and rich. I'm going to want seconds for sure."

"Girl, give yourself a pat on the back," Sienna said in agreement. Micah stirred and whimpered, causing her to eat her food faster. She knew what that meant.

"Look at you eating like you're being chased." Jade giggled.

Jade had placed a generous slice of chicken breast and brussels sprouts on her plate. Sienna didn't know how the other woman resisted all the food she prepared.

"Let me tell you—motherhood is not for the faint of heart. It's a full-time job. This little guy gets all my attention. I can't concentrate on anything else when he's awake." Sienna sighed. "I'm exhausted at the end of the day, and I've only been with him a few days."

"Whew. You guys are giving me flashbacks. I'm leaving all that to you both." Jade pointed at Kelsey and Sienna. "It's been quite a few years, but I haven't forgotten how I was with Izzy. Trying to breastfeed while working was no joke. If it weren't for you guys, I wouldn't have made it back then."

"We were happy to help." Kelsey yawned on cue. "I'm glad Zach is home to help me with the girls, or I would go bananas." She wiped her mouth and held her plate out for Sienna to get her more potatoes. But Jade volunteered, returning with napkins for the both of them. "Sasha has taken over my clients because my feet started swelling up during house-showings." Sasha was Kelsey's assistant at her real estate business.

Sienna bobbed her head. "That's a smart move." Her braids swung in her face, and she moved them out the way. There had been a few times when she had been feeding Micah and that happened. Maybe it was time to take them out or shorten them. Plus, she was thinking about trimming her nails. Sienna didn't want to scratch the baby by accident.

"I didn't want to, but my son is worth the sacrifice." Kelsey exhaled and her face was a snapshot of contentment, but Sienna was stuck on one word.

Sacrifice. Sienna looked at Micah, who was now stretching. She was used to doing her own thing, when and how she wanted. Becoming a mother would change all that. Doubt churned in her belly. She didn't know if she was ready. She had her career, and she was enjoying the single lifestyle, coming and going as she pleased. Suddenly, Micah's face got squishy, and he released a wail. Sienna moved the tray, scooped him into her arms and held him against her chest. And her misgivings washed away like a sandcastle at the beach. Yes, she could do this. One day. Not too soon. But not far either.

Joel texted that he was five minutes away. She sent him a thumbs-up emoji back.

Jade jumped up. "Something tells me we might not get to this movie today." She dug into the diaper bag and went to prepare Micah's bottle.

Sienna shook her head. "We're going to watch this film even if we we're here until midnight."

"Do you need me to hold him so you can finish eating?" Kelsey asked, holding out a hand.

"No. I'm good. I want to limit the number of people in close contact with him until he gets his shots tomorrow. I'll box up the rest of my food. Joel should be here in a few minutes to relieve me." Sienna wiped her mouth and reached into her purse for a handheld mirror to check her face. When she looked up, she noticed that both Kelsey and Jade had their eyes pinned on her. "Would you two quit studying me like I'm a specimen under a microscope?"

"You don't see what we're seeing. You're getting all dolled up for Joel," Kelsey said.

"Give me a break. I just finished eating. It's called good hygiene."

"Okay, tell yourself that if it makes you feel better," Jade teased.

Sienna cut her eyes and focused on Micah. Her two friends needed to stop with all that nonsense. She wasn't trying to get fixed up because Joel was coming. It was just plain old Joel, after all. He had known her through her braces and acne phases.

The doorbell rang. If her heart rate escalated, it was because she knew Micah would be excited to see his uncle. No other reason.

At least, that's what she told herself…

Joel rushed through the door of the doctor's office—ten minutes late—with a wailing baby in his arms and his shirt covered in spit-up. Sienna was already there, waiting, when he arrived. She was the only one in the waiting room, which meant he might still be able to see the doctor today. The sun rays were bright through the half-open blinds, lighting up the otherwise dim space. There was a huge outer space mural on the wall in front of him, with lots of stars and a stork at the center, holding a baby.

She shot to her feet and placed a hand on her hip. "You're late."

"Not right now, okay? Please." Joel passed Micah to her.

Wrinkling her nose, she took the infant and patted him on the back. "Ugh. He's a mess." Once Micah was in her arms, he stopped crying. Figures. She snatched the diaper bag off his shoulder, and he rushed over to the receptionist to check in.

"I'm sorry I'm late. It was a rough morning with my nephew," he huffed, wiping his face and getting puke on his cheek.

The receptionist gave him a sympathetic look and handed him a baby wipe. "It's okay. We understand. Just breathe. There are two people ahead of you, so let's get Micah registered to be seen. Do you have his insurance information?"

Her calm demeanor made Joel's stomach muscles relax. He dabbed at his face. "His father told me that he filled out the paperwork in advance online, and he emailed a copy of the insurance card to you."

"Okay. Let me check."

While she searched the records, he glanced over to see Sienna looking at him with fire in her eyes. She had already undressed Micah and was cleaning him with a baby wipe. He wanted to tell her there was a restroom which probably had a changing table but she didn't look like she would welcome his input.

"I've found it. Everything looks to be in order," the receptionist said. "You can have a seat and wait for Dr. McPherson to call you back."

He traipsed back over to join Sienna, preparing himself, knowing she had been waiting to fuss with him.

She gave him a jab. "What happened? I've been here for a half hour waiting for you. I hate lateness. It's my pet peeve."

"That makes two of us."

She snorted. "You have a funny way of showing it."

"Will you ease up on me?" he said, his voice rising. "I'm new at this. I miscalculated the amount of time needed to get myself plus Micah ready."

"Didn't you see the outfit I put out for him before I left last night?" she asked in a less frosty tone, like she was a tiny bit less irritated with him.

"Yes, thank you. I'm also grateful you restocked his bag and prepped a couple bottles." He exhaled. "You're the best thing that has happened to Micah besides his parents."

"Hey. Don't be so hard on yourself," Sienna said gently. "Not many people would have offered to care for a newborn full-time. They would have seen it as a big inconvenience. Micah is blessed to have you in his life."

Joel turned to face her, touching her arm. "That means a lot, coming from you."

"Well, you know I wouldn't say it if it weren't true." She gave Micah a light kiss on the forehead.

His sense of humor kicked in. "I wonder if it's going to hail or snow today."

She frowned. "It's June 10th. I know summer doesn't officially begin until the 21st, but I would say it has already begun."

"Yes, but you're being nice to me. Makes me wonder if something wonky is about to happen. Like maybe the earth might fall off its axis or something."

She responded with a haughty, "I won't dignify that with a response." But he thought he saw her lips quirk.

The door opened, and the physician's assistant called out for Micah Armstrong. Gathering their belongings, Sienna and Joel followed her down a short hallway to a room bearing the number three. She ushered them inside the small brightly lit room, keeping up a steady chatter while she undressed and weighed Micah, took his temperature, and measured his height. Micah wiggled the entire time, but he didn't cry. In fact, the PA was charmed by his bright eyes.

There was a stool and an armchair. Joel directed Sienna to sit while he perched against the wall across from the examining table.

Once she had recorded the vitals and set up the instruments and supplies the doctor would need, she said, "Dr. McPherson will be with you shortly," then left the room.

Joel went over to where Micah lay only in his diaper. The infant's lower lip was trembling.

Sienna, who was wearing in a tangerine-colored sundress, rubbed her arms. "I can't believe she left him naked like that. It's cold in here. Imagine the irony of catching a cold at the doctor's office. If he gets sick, I am going to be furious."

Sienna fussed like any mother would, which made Joel smile. He reached for the blanket and covered Micah. "That's better."

After a light rap on the door, Dr. McPherson entered. "Who do we have here?" he asked after greeting Joel and Sienna. He donned a fresh pair of latex gloves, approached Micah and began the physical, asking about Micah's immunization history.

"He had his first hepatitis shot after birth."

"Okay, I'm going to give him his second hepatitis shot today since he is now a month old. You'll want to set up an appointment for him to get his next set of shots about three to four weeks from now." The doctor tore the plastic wrapping and took out the needle.

As soon as Joel saw the needle, he placed a hand on the wall, feeling light-headed. He couldn't do this. Dr. McPherson hummed a tune, as if he wasn't getting ready to puncture Micah. Joel rested his head on his hands. It was too much.

Joel felt a hand on his back and tensed. He had forgotten Sienna was in the room. She had remained quiet the entire time.

"Are you going to be all right?" she asked.

"Why wouldn't I be?" From the corner of his eye, he could see the doctor hovering over Micah with that dangerous weapon in his hand. Joel's heart thumped in his chest.

"Do you want to wait outside?" Sienna whispered.

"Naw. I'm good. I've got to be here for Micah." His chest was now heaving, and his armpits were sweating despite the coolness in the air. But he made himself face Micah. Meanwhile, the doctor was now whistling, ignoring them. He was probably used to terrified parents and had learned to tune them out.

Sienna hovered close. "Listen, go sit down because if you fall, I'm stepping out of the way, and you'll hit the floor."

Joel's mouth dropped. "That's cold."

"I'm not about to try to break your fall and get injured in the process."

"All right, here we go, little guy." The doctor held Micah still and lifted the needle.

Hyperventilating, Joel yelled, "Stop! Stop! You're going to hurt him and make him cry. I won't let you do it."

Sienna gasped and covered her mouth before she smirked. He clenched his lips to keep from snapping at her because he knew she was going to tease him about this later. But he was too distraught to care.

Dr. McPherson's eyes went wide. "Maybe you need to wait outside." His eyes were friendly, but his voice was firm. Joel knew he had to get it together. Fast.

"No, no. I apologize." He wrapped his arms around himself. "I know I'm overreacting, but I don't want to see my nephew get hurt, and I can't stand the sight of needles." Micah, who had no idea what was about to happen to him, was busy sucking on his hand. Poor little guy was clueless.

"I don't want to see that either," the doctor said in a calm tone. "That's why I need to give him this immunization."

Joel gave a little nod, and the doctor proceeded. To Joel's surprise, Sienna held his hand and squeezed it. He swallowed. "You intend to gloat over this?"

"I probably will later. But not now."

He squeezed his eyes shut and tried not to envision that thin piece of metal piercing his nephew's skin. Joel gritted his teeth when Micah wailed at the intrusion. "Hold on, Micah. It's going to be all right." He repeated those words more for his own benefit than for Micah's, and then he held his breath.

"All done."

Joel's eyes popped open, and his shoulders slumped. He could breathe again. Tears slid down both his and Micah's cheeks.

The doctor placed a Band-Aid on the injection site, once again ignoring Joel's theatrics. "Micah might be fussy or show symptoms like fatigue or stomach problems. If his symptoms go beyond a day, reach out," he said, then headed out the door to inflict more damage on another unsuspecting baby or toddler.

Joel looked over at Sienna, and his mouth dropped open. She was holding a camera with her free hand.

"I can't believe you recorded this." He wiped the tears from his face with a tissue.

She laughed, not in the least bit apologetic. "I had to. It isn't every day I get to see the perfect Joel Armstrong bested by a hypodermic needle." She put her phone away and went to get Micah dressed, moving fast, like she had done it many times before.

"You'd make a great mom," he said.

"I know."

He raised a brow. "Okay, someone's confident."

She shrugged. "Just telling the truth. I pride myself on doing my best, and if I were to become a mother, I would read all the books I could and reach out to the older moms in the church for advice. Plus, my girls would have my back—so yes, I would be a great mother." She bundled Micah in his blanket and motioned for Joel to open the door.

Picking up the diaper bag, Joel asked, "So why haven't you?"

"Need to be married." She scurried ahead to Joel's Jeep.

"Why aren't you married?"

"Don't have a contender."

"Why not?"

She released a sound of exasperation. "Haven't found the One, haven't been looking and not about to start." She spoke with finality, squelching Joel's next question.

"Sorry." He opened the back seat door, and Sienna reached over to strap Micah into the car seat.

She gazed down at Micah, her voice tender, her smile sweet. "He's so precious."

"Agreed," Joel said, tamping down a sudden, inexplicable wish: that Sienna would look at him without bitterness or irritation. Pushing that ridiculous notion aside, he said, "The right husband is out there for you, you know."

Sienna's attention remained pinned on Micah. "Yep. And when I find him, I'm going from hello to honeymoon." She reached over to hold Micah's tiny hand. "Right, little man? One day, I'll be a mom to a sweetie just like you."

Micah returned Sienna's gaze with such trust that Joel's heart constricted. A new desire pierced his being that petrified and thrilled him at the same time. A desire to be a father to a child one day. To earn a child's trust and unconditional love and to bestow it in return. He gripped the car door while new sensations rocked his core. For once, Joel and Sienna had something in common, but this was something he knew he wouldn't share. He couldn't bear it if she laughed at him—or worse, told him he wasn't worthy of such a role. And that he never would be.

Chapter Five

Sienna stood in her kitchen, finishing up her muffin, and frowned. It was a little past 7:30 a.m., and she had been about to head over to Joel's house when her mother called on FaceTime. The second call in a matter of days. It was not like her mother to call again so soon. Their mother-daughter talks were usually few and far between by mutual consent. Daphne couldn't engage in a conversation without bringing up her sister, Sage, and Sienna couldn't continue that discussion without feeling the guilt. Guilt for being alive when her sister wasn't. Much to her parents' regret.

So the fact that Daphne was calling again could only mean one thing: something was wrong with her dad. Sienna's stomach knotted.

"Mom, what's going on?" When her mother hesitated, Sienna dropped into the chair and pressed. "Mom, what is it? What is it? You've got to tell me."

Daphne drew in a deep breath. "I just found out I have hemochromatosis."

"Hema—what?"

"Hemochromatosis. It's when you absorb too much iron from food. Iron can build up in the tissues in your body and settle in the liver." She spoke in a clear, concise manner, evidence she had done her research. "I've had a lot of joint pain lately and some hair loss, so I went to see my primary care physician. He referred me to a specialist, and after some blood work, I got my diagnosis today." Daphne looked away from the screen. "He wants to do some more tests." She swallowed. "It might be more…serious."

Her grave words made Sienna's chest tighten. She stood. "That's it. I'm driving up there. If I leave now, I'll be there by midafternoon."

Her parents had moved to Pittsburgh, which was five hours away. She would arrive by early afternoon if she left now… Maybe Joel would let her take Micah with her on the journey. Or maybe Jade would step in for a few days.

"When is your next appointment?" she asked. "Since I'm on break, I can stay with you for as long as you need."

Daphne held up a hand. "No, don't come. Let me hear what the doctor has to say first. Besides, I have a performance today, and I won't make good company."

Sienna's brows rose to her hairline. "You're still doing shows?"

Her mother was a gifted harpist and jazz singer who performed to sold-out crowds. In fact, Sienna came from a family of talents. Her sister, Sage, had been a child prodigy, an extraordinary pianist since the age of three. But Sage had died in her sleep at fifteen when Sienna was five years old, for no reason that the coroner could identify. Sienna believed that was why her parents' grief felt as fresh as the day they'd discovered Sage's lifeless body.

"I have to." Daphne's lips quivered. "The show must go on. People paid good money to see me, and I can't disappoint them. Plus, it makes me feel close to Sage."

Sienna's heart twisted. She wanted to yell, to plead that she was still here, alive, and she needed her mother's attention. But she swallowed her pain and jealousy and gave her a jerky nod. Her parents had always told Sienna how sweet and smart Sage was. They'd never seemed satisfied with Sienna. Daphne and Lennox King couldn't understand why Sienna couldn't sing or play an instrument or why she hadn't followed Lennox's path as an entertainment lawyer.

Daphne hung up after that, stating she had to prepare breakfast for herself and Sienna's father. Like it was still a normal day. Like she wasn't facing the possibility of having a serious disease.

At that realization, Sienna fell apart. Outside, the sun was bright and beaming, its heat already searing her arms through the kitchen window. The exact opposite of how she was feeling on the inside.

Now more than ever, Sienna had to pass her dissertation defense. Make her mother proud. In fact, Sienna vowed to call Daphne more often. She looked at her kitchen clock, and her eyes widened. It was close to nine. For a split second, Sienna thought about contacting Joel to tell him she couldn't make it. But then she thought of her mother, who was still working, and Micah's cute little face, and that propelled her to her feet.

Whispering one of her favorite scriptures—"I will

look to the hills from when cometh my help"—Sienna grabbed her keys and rushed through the door.

Sienna was quiet. Too quiet.

Since her arrival, she hadn't uttered one insult. Instead, after a whispered *good morning*, she had taken Micah out of his arms and then gone to sit on the couch to rock the baby. In between rocking, she was reading something on her phone. Every now and then, he heard a sharp intake of breath. And then, nothing.

Joel prepared the baby bottle. From her position on the couch, Sienna should have been able to see when he poured in too much formula since his house was open concept. And she had to have seen him spill it when he tried pouring it back in the bottle. Yet she said nothing.

He put the bottle in the microwave before remembering the warmer. Yanking the microwave door open, he snatched the bottle, the milk sloshing his hand, and put it to warm.

Still nothing.

That spooked him, which made him nervous.

Joel much preferred the chatty, slightly condescending woman over this...eerie, docile person. But then, he considered that this might be Sienna's way of ensuring they kept their truce and relaxed. Somewhat.

Until he heard a sniffle.

Joel tensed. Something was definitely wrong, but maybe he needed to mind his business. Sienna could be prickly, and he wasn't in the mood to get snapped at. Then he heard another sniffle, and yet another, and he knew he couldn't leave for work without making sure she was okay. He inched his way closer to her. She was humming a tune to Micah. This time there was a hiccup. Joel sat next to her and gathered the courage to take her hand. She stiffened but didn't push him away.

"What's wrong?" he asked in a gentle tone.

"Nothing I want to talk about with you." Right after saying those words, she squeezed his hand. He doubted she realized she had done so, but that gesture was a sure sign that she needed to release whatever was troubling her.

"Believe it or not, I can be a good sounding board. I can listen without saying a word, if that's what you need."

Sienna kept her eyes focused on the baby. "I just learned my mother has too much iron in her blood, and the doctors want her to do more tests. I might be overreacting, but my mother said it was serious. Serious to me means life-threatening."

Hearing the fear in Sienna's voice, compassion pierced his core like a target on a bull's-eye. "Oh, Sienna. I'm so sorry to hear this." Memories of losing his own parents surfaced. "Do you need to go home? I can take off today or see if I can take Micah with me." However, his office was no place for a baby. "Or I can work virtually."

She shook her head. "If it's okay with you, I need to be here. Micah is a soothing distraction." She cooed at the baby. "Just holding him is already a big help."

He rubbed the bridge of his nose. "If you're sure…" He half stood before sitting back down. He didn't feel right leaving.

She nodded, still not looking his way. "Yes, this is the only thing today I am sure of. I know I won't be able to work on my dissertation." She shooed him with a wave. "Go. Go to work. I'll be okay."

If she said she was fine, he needed to respect that. Besides, he had to get to the office. As the new associate editor, Joel needed to set a good example for the junior editors. He didn't want them to see him being tardy and think it was okay for them to do the same. Joel jumped to his feet and walked to the front door. His hand gripped the handle, and he hesitated. Turning around, he asked, "Can Kelsey or Jade stop by?"

She finally met his eyes. "I'm good, Joel. I don't need babysitting." She sounded like her old self, but her face said something different. Her eyes were red, her face puffy, and his heart melted.

That did it. Joel walked toward her. "I'll stay for a little bit." He sent Kelsey and Jade a text asking them to come over. Kelsey gave him a thumbs-up while Jade texted to say she would be over in twenty. Joel looked at his watch. He could wait until they arrived before heading off to work.

Sienna got up, snuggling Micah close, and sauntered into the kitchen to get the baby's bottle. Joel rushed to her side to take Micah from her arms. Micah scrunched his face and released a small whimper.

Sienna tested the milk on her wrist. "It's a little too warm." She screwed the cap on and then went to run cold water on the bottle. Micah fussed before letting out a wail, his bottom lip quivering in fury.

Watching his face redden, Joel panicked. "Hurry up."

"Relax. Babies cry. It's what they do."

"Well, he's doing a good job at it." Joel scrambled to hold the squirmy infant, who then stiffened his legs, bunch his fists and cried. Joel's heart thumped from his nerves, but Sienna looked unbothered, her face calm. He admired how she was able to push her own grief aside to care for Micah.

Sienna tested the milk on her wrist and then gave Joel a nod. He handed over the baby and sighed with relief. Once she plopped the bottle in Micah's mouth, the baby stopped mid-cry.

"See? There now. It's okay. It's okay." She soothed him while walking back over to the couch. Micah gurgled greedily as she caressed his tiny head.

Then the doorbell rang. Joel rushed to let Kelsey inside. She greeted Joel with a quick hug. "I came as soon as I dropped the twins at day camp."

"I told you I didn't need babysitting," Sienna snapped at him.

"Excuse me for being worried," Joel fumed, going to the refrigerator to pull out his sandwich and bottle of water. He started packing his lunch, not knowing why he even bothered trying to be nice to this woman or show concern.

"I prayed for your mother in my morning prayers," Kelsey said—probably to divert another possible argument.

Joel zipped up his lunch bag and stood a few feet away from them listening in on the conversation.

"Thank you," Sienna muttered. "But I didn't want to put you out. I know you're busy with the girls in the mornings."

"Nonsense," Kelsey said, settling beside Sienna. "This isn't any trouble. I don't have any appointments scheduled so I'm good."

Her shoulders slumped and the tears began to fall. Kelsey wrapped her arms around Sienna. Joel retrieved Micah from Sienna's arms and patted his back to burp him. Micah's head lolled like he was ready to sleep. Holding the baby in one arm, Joel went to his bedroom to retrieve the bassinet and then positioned it beside Sienna by the couch. Then he lowered the now sleeping infant inside and wrapped a blanket around him.

By this time, Sienna's cries had subdued to sniffles as Kelsey rocked her back and forth. Watching them, Joel knew he had made the right decision contacting her friends—the Three Amigas, as they called themselves.

The screen door creaked, and then Jade stepped over the threshold. "Hey, peoples!"

"Shh…" Kelsey said, twisting her body, with a finger over her mouth. "You'll wake the baby."

Jade's eyes widened. "Oh. I'm sorry." She moved to close the front door, but Joel gestured to her to leave it open. Jade tiptoed into the room and sat on Sienna's other side, resting her head on Sienna's shoulder.

"You guys really shouldn't have come," Sienna protested, though she snuggled closer to her friends.

With a small smile, Joel knew this was his cue. Before he walked out the front door, Joel gave the three friends a backward glance, admiring their connection. He couldn't help but recall his mother's passing and how he and his brother had been estranged during that time. Joel had spent hours alone, dealing with his grief, before deciding to reach out to his brother.

Greg had ignored his attempts at communication at first. Both Joel and Greg were loners, letting few people in their circle. It had taken some effort, but eventually, Joel was able to have a long-distance relationship with Greg, with the occasional phone call sprinkled in. If Tessa hadn't gotten sick, Joel didn't know when he would have ventured out to Shreveport to see his sibling. That knowledge shamed him.

Joel entered the vehicle and slammed the door shut. As he gripped the wheel, he thought of the three girlfriends inside and their bond. And Greg and Tessa's bond. They all had someone to lean on. Joel didn't have that. Truth was, if he died today, not too many people would care. That punched him in the gut.

His cell pinged with a message from his boss, jarring him back to the present. Joel pushed the malaise out of his mind and drove to the office. But the thought refused to leave, festering in his psyche. For the first time, he noticed all the picture frames on the desks of his coworkers. Family. Smiling faces.

Then he walked into his new large office and looked at his degrees posted on the wall. There were also a few pictures of Joel with the odd celebrity or some journalism award. He had framed some memorable articles he'd written, but nowhere did he see photos of him with family or friends.

He was lonely. His life was lacking. Then he thought of Micah. The little guy brought a smile to Joel's face and warmed his heart. For the time being, he wasn't alone, and Joel would soak up all this time with his nephew, who had already found a place in his heart. Yes, it was short-term, but he wouldn't dwell on that.

Pulling up a picture of Micah on his computer screen, Joel printed out a color copy. With a great amount of satisfaction, Joel rearranged the frames on the wall and placed his nephew at the center. Sitting in his swivel chair, Joel placed his hands behind his head and focused on his nephew's face. For the first time, Joel felt something he had never experienced on a deeper level.

A sense of belonging.

A sense of purpose.

Micah was dependent on Joel for all his needs, and Joel resolved not to let his nephew down. Until Micah reunited with his parents, Joel would fill his life with all the love he had to give.

Chapter Six

"Mom, please stop giving out my phone number to random people," Sienna begged Daphne on the phone. She had been about to fall asleep when she heard her mother's ring tone. Though Micah had tuckered her out that day, Sienna had answered her mother's call.

Daphne held up a finger. "I'd like to see you settled down and married, just in case…"

Her heart twisted. "Mom, you're not going anywhere anytime soon. I refuse to believe that. No one knows what God can do. Let's wait to see what the doctor says."

"I'm just being realistic. Which is why I'm helping you find a partner. Just like back in the olden days."

Sienna squinted. Her mother seemed like a stranger to her at the moment. She looked and sounded like Daphne King, but the words did not. "Are you for real right now, Mom? I don't need help when it comes to men. I'm just not interested. Right now, I'm all for God, for life," she said, speaking the mantra of the Three Amigas. That slogan was something Sienna, Kelsey and Jade had come up with in their twenties.

"I'm all for being all for God but you don't have to be all alone for life." Her mother gave a small smile and then coughed. "It's good to have someone by your side. It's okay to have help. I don't know how I would go through all this without Lennox. In the Bible, Isaac trusted his father to choose his wife, so you can do the same for me."

Sienna's mouth popped open. "Mom, I know you're not using the Bible to get your way."

She sat up in bed. She was having a hard time processing her mother's sudden shift from education to love—although Daphne wasn't necessarily talking about love. It was all about finding someone suitable, someone who met with her mother's approval. Not Sienna's, judging from her mother's choices.

"Whatever it takes." Her mother didn't appear the least bit sorry.

"Okay, but I've heard from a surgeon, an oncologist and a nurse within days of each other. Where are you finding these men?" She couldn't picture her mother scrolling through a dating site. Just then, Joel texted her a picture of her feeding Micah a bottle earlier in the day. *Aw.*

She quickly sent back a heart emoji before returning her attention to the conversation with her mother.

Daphne's lips quirked. "They are all handsome and upstanding men I met when I was going to doctor's appointments at the medical center. I'm sure you would like one of them if you gave them a chance. I already vetted them for you." She held up her fingers and counted off. "All three men have all their teeth. Their parents are still together. And they have credit scores in the eight hundreds."

Sienna slapped her forehead. "Mom, how do you know all that? And why is it important they have all their teeth? That is such random criteria." For some reason, Joel's perfect whites came to mind, but she blinked that image away before it imprinted in her brain.

"Oh, I have my ways," Daphne said. "If a man takes the time to tend to his dental health, he will take the time to properly care for you."

Sienna half expected her mother to laugh, but Daphne seemed totally serious. "But Mom, Dad has had a lot of dental work in recent years." She shook her head at the weird thread of conversation.

"Never mind that. Your father had all of his teeth when we met, and he's done me right all these years. That's what counts."

Okay, she had to halt this, snip this vine before it got out of control. "If and when I'm ready to date, it will be someone of *my* choice." For some reason, Joel popped into her mind again, but she attributed it to the fact that he had agreed to be her fake wedding date. Tossing her braids out of her face, Sienna continued. "I'm too focused on getting my dissertation done to worry about dating. Earning my doctorate is my main concern. It used to be all you talked about as well, so this one-eighty turn is throwing me off."

"I know I've pushed you and continue to push you, but I want what all mothers want," Daphne said. "For you to be better than I was. I hope you know that was always my motivation."

Sienna detected a hint of an apology somewhere weaved into those words. "I know, Mom, thanks," she said.

"I feel the same," a deep bass voice, belonging to her

father said over the phone. He must have heard her mother and decided to chime in.

"Hi, Dad," Sienna said.

"We love you, baby girl," Lennox said. "Your mom and I are blessed to have you."

Overwhelmed, Sienna could only shake her head. "Why now?" she asked.

"Because this experience is teaching us that life is short, and we are learning how vital it is to let the people you love know what they mean to you while we can." He choked on the words.

"I need to come see you. I should be there with you."

"Please, honey. Wait until after my appointment and then...we'll see," her mom said. "I like knowing you're out there living your life. For now, let's agree to talk every day." A sob broke through her words. "I'm sorry, honey, I wish I could stay and talk. But I've got to go." Daphne ended the call.

Sienna broke down. Her shoulders shook, and she struggled to breathe. She uttered heartfelt prayers to God. "I can't lose her, Lord. Not yet." Her heart ached. She finally seemed to have gained her parents' acceptance, something she had always wanted. Something she would trade in an instant if it meant more time with her mother.

Greg's wife wasn't getting better. But at least she hadn't gotten worse.

"I'm glad to hear Tessa's stable," Joel said, talking to his brother early the next morning as he sat against the headboard on his king-size bed.

Greg had called him just before sunrise, but Joel was already awake because Micah had needed changing and feeding. From his spot on the bed, he had two large windows to his left and another to the right of the bed, which allowed a lot of sunlight to enter the room since Joel had forgotten to lower the blinds the night before. He glanced through one of the windows, admiring the various hues of orange and yellow while the sun rose. The temperature was already seventy-three degrees; the day was going to be a scorcher. He was thankful for the clear skies.

"Yes, this is good news." Greg sounded relieved. "What's Micah doing?"

Lowering his head to look at Micah lying next to him, Joel grinned when he saw those bright eyes staring back. "He's right here beside me, making the most adorable sounds." Micah kicked his little legs and cooed, making Joel laugh.

Sienna would be real upset with him if she saw that Micah wasn't using the bassinet. Not that she would yell or say something snappy. Nope. She would grit her teeth and suggest that he use the bassinet through a forced smile. He chuckled at the image. Even though he had told her to still be her snarky self around him, she was convinced they could go without arguing, mumbling that it was best for Micah. Joel had agreed, but he didn't think the truce was possible.

"I wish I could hold him. I miss my son, and I feel guilty that he's not here." Greg choked up. "It's just that Tessa really needs me. I haven't left her side except to shower and eat."

Joel's heart constricted when he heard the longing in his brother's voice. He was quick to reassure him. "You're doing the right thing. Micah's an infant. He doesn't know, and he won't remember if you are here. When he's older and you tell him the story, he's going to think you're an amazing husband and father."

"I hope so…" Greg sounded better but still unsure.

"I know so. In the meantime, I'm honored that you chose me as a stand-in." Joel rubbed Micah's tummy. "This sweet boy has been wonderful so far."

"I was so scared to call and ask you for help," Greg admitted. "I didn't think you'd answer the phone, especially since you'd been trying to reach me for weeks, and I hadn't answered… I'm sorry about that, by the way."

Just then Micah stiffened and scrunched his face. Joel knew what that meant.

"I understand," Joel said, trying to ignore the grunting sounds beside him. "It had been years since we saw each other. But we're family. Our parents are gone, and we're the only ones left. You're all the family I have—correction, *had*. Now I get to count Micah."

After a few moments of quiet, Greg said, "Thanks. It meant a lot that you jumped on a plane to be here to offer your support."

"I was glad to be of help, and I wanted to be there for you," Joel said.

Greg chuckled. "I know you didn't expect to leave saddled with a newborn."

"I'm having the time of my life." Joel started at the realization of how true that actually was. Yes, he was lacking sleep, and Micah needed a lot of attention, but Joel had fallen for the little guy. "Hang on a sec." He switched their call to video. Greg needed to see Micah. Seconds later, Joel saw his brother's face. Greg had dark circles under his eyes. His beard had grown in, and he needed a haircut. "It's good to see you."

Greg nodded, laughed and patted his head. "I know, I'm far from camera-ready..."

"You have more important things to worry about."

"Yes, but I'd better schedule an appointment with my barber. If Tessa wakes up and sees me..." Greg trailed off.

"*When* Tessa wakes up, she is going to be too happy to see you to care about your grooming. Let me show you Micah." Joel angled the phone so that Greg could see his son.

Greg interacted with Micah for about ten minutes before Micah began to get fussy. "I've got to get him cleaned up. But how about I call later so you and Tessa can visit with him?"

His brother nodded with enthusiasm. "That's a great idea. Talk to you soon."

Once they disconnected, Joel scooped the baby in his arms and headed into the nursery. He used his watch to start a timer. After placing Micah on the changing table, Joel grabbed wipes, cleaned him up and put on a fresh diaper all in four minutes and thirty-two seconds. He pumped his fists. This was his best time yet. He was determined to get it under three minutes.

Joel headed downstairs to the living room and activated the swing. Once he strapped Micah in the way Sienna had shown him, Joel went to put coffee on and prepare the baby's bottle. Just as he started the bottle warmer, he heard the lock click, and seconds later, Sienna walked inside. She went over to greet Micah and played with his toes before turning to face Joel.

"Looks like you're having a good morning," she said with a smile.

This was the first time she had used the spare key Joel had given her. "I changed Micah's diaper in under five minutes this morning." He couldn't wait to brag.

She was dressed in a floral top, yellow capris and sandals, and she came toward him with a determined look in her eyes and a box of Patty's Pretzels in one hand. "That's nothing. I can change him in four minutes."

He lifted his brows. "Must we compete over everything? Can't you just congratulate me?" The coffee began to brew, and his stomach growled. He reached into the cabinet for two mugs.

"Congratulations, but I still beat you." She ambled over to the counter and rested the pretzels on the counter. His mouth was already watering for the almond or cinnamon flavor. Sienna then lifted the bottle out of the warmer to check the temperature before putting it back to warm. Joel didn't bother to tell her that he had just placed it inside, because she would have still checked anyway.

"If I didn't want to waste a perfectly good diaper, I would challenge you to a standoff."

"No need. Micah will need changing soon enough, and I will record my time." He peered over her shoulder to see what kind of pretzels she had purchased, but Sienna slapped his hand.

Joel chuckled and switched topics. "How is your mother doing?"

Facing him, her eyes dimmed. "She's being practical, as always. Still trying to plan my life." She lowered her head, tucking her chin toward her chest, rubbing the edge of the sandal on the floor.

For a few minutes, the only sounds in the room were the gurgling of the coffee maker and the bottle warmer. Joel waited, thinking she would elaborate, but Sienna was focused on getting Micah's bottle ready. Joel looked over to see that Micah had fallen asleep.

"That bottle will have to wait." He gestured toward the swing.

Sienna placed the bottle on the counter and opened the bottle sanitizer to retrieve the cap. Each night, Joel cleaned the bottles as Sienna had directed him. He poured their coffee and carried their steaming mugs to the kitchen table. Sienna retrieved two plates from the cupboard before coming over to join him with the pretzels.

"What did you mean when you said your mother's still trying to plan your life?" he dared to ask, unsure if she would answer. Then he snatched an almond pretzel and bit into it.

Sienna shrugged and took a sip of her coffee. "She's trying to find me a husband before she goes. One with perfect teeth and even more perfect credit." She lifted a hand. "And one whose parents are still married."

His brows rose. "Wow. Your mom is a trip." Joel didn't remember her parents all that well. If he recalled, the Kings had rarely shown up to any of the school events, and when they did come, they had been standoffish. He set the mug down hard enough for the contents to slosh over and onto the table.

"A trip and a half."

They both reached for the paper towels at the same

time, their hands colliding. He felt a spark from the contact and pulled his hand away immediately. Sienna tore off enough to blot the mess off the wooden table.

"Did you tell her about us?" He took another sip of his coffee.

Sienna's brows furrowed, and her lips tightened. "What do you mean by *us*? There is no us, so don't get it twisted. We have an arrangement." Just like that, her tone was frosty. As frosty as the icing on the cinnamon pretzel she grabbed.

"I know that there is no us, and for that, I am very relieved," he shot back. "But if you wanted her to stop setting you up with random guys, you could have told her you were already dating me." He didn't add that he met all her mother's requirements: his teeth and credit were flawless. And his parents had been together until their untimely death when his childhood home had caught fire. Instead of running out of the house, both had tried to save their belongings.

"I did think of saying that, but I didn't want to get her hopes up for nothing. Knowing my mom, she would want to meet you, interrogate you—although the thought of you facing an inquisition sounds like fun—and I didn't want to open that can of worms. But I'll make sure to tell her that the next time we talk, especially since she has these random men reaching out to me. That would put her mind at ease and give me breathing room to finish prepping for my defense."

"Glad to be of service. Let me know if I can help with your dissertation." He reached for another pretzel, choosing the only one with a hot dog in it, and tried not to dwell on the random men contacting Sienna.

Sienna snatched the pretzel out of his hand. "Sorry, this one's for me. It was the only one in the case."

He ripped off half of the pretzel and popped it into his mouth.

Her eyes blazed. "I can't believe you would do that. There is another almond for you."

Joel shrugged. "I wanted that one."

"You could have asked me for half." She bit into the pretzel and started chewing with a vengeance.

"You wouldn't have given it to me."

"You're right about that."

"Well, that's why I took it."

"You're too childish for words. I can't with you." The chair scraped as she stood and stormed over to toss the empty pretzel wrappers in the trash. Then she went over to where Micah was sleeping.

"It's just a pretzel," he called out, gathering their mugs and placing them in the sink.

"It was mine."

"Well, now it's ours. My stomach quite enjoyed it." He started to leave the kitchen.

She pointed at him. "You'd better wash those cups."

He glared at her. "Don't tell me what to do in my house."

Sienna lifted her chin. "I just did. If you leave them, who do you think is going to wash them?"

He placed his hands on his hips. "Me. When I get home."

She pinned him with an icy glare. "In the time you spend arguing with me, you would have already been done."

"This isn't about the cups. This is about the pretzel."

Joel rubbed his temples. He couldn't believe they were already going at it. Over pretzels.

"No. This is about you thinking just of yourself."

He opened his mouth to argue when her words hit him. He released a huge breath of air. "You're right. I should have asked you before taking the pretzel." Even as he spoke the words, Joel wondered why he was always the one apologizing, but he tamped down the rebellious thought and continued with his apology. "I'm used to looking out just for me. I'm not used to sharing." He looked Micah's way. "But it isn't just about me. Not anymore."

Sienna walked over and stood before him, and Joel was struck by her beauty. He frowned, chiding himself for that observation and reminding himself that the person inside the pretty package was as prickly as a porcupine. He steeled himself for what she would say next, but she surprised him.

Clasping her hands, she looked up at him from under her lashes. "Maybe I overreacted as well. I'm sorry too. Tell you what—tomorrow, I'll order two of those in advance before I come over."

Joel so wanted to respond with "Don't bother" or "No need," but he realized he enjoyed sparring with Sienna too much and needed to accept her peace offering with grace. So he said, "That would be wonderful. Thank you."

Neither mentioned the sparkle of something that flared between them. But Joel had felt it, and that stayed with him all day.

Chapter Seven

There was nothing better than a summer clearance sale. Sienna and Jade had decided to drive down to the outlet mall early the next morning. Joel was off that day and would take care of Micah while she searched for suitable wedding attire. Sienna needed at least five dresses for the three weddings she would attend. She liked to have two backup dresses in case she arrived at the wedding and the bridal party was in the same color scheme, or someone else was wearing the same dress.

The women stood across from each other in a boutique, going through dresses. They had already found a couple for Jade, but Sienna was picky. She needed spunky colors, designs that accentuated her figure and plenty of sparkle. Pizazz. Unlike Jade—who had preordered her dresses online, so all she had to do was pick them up—Sienna's shopping strategy was an *I'll know it when I see it* approach. That was why Kelsey had declined tagging along for what could easily turn into an all-day affair.

"I still can't believe you're going to this wedding

with Joel." A wedding that was in two days. An evening wedding, according to the invite, and one that asked the guests to don masks because of the *Phantom of the Opera* theme. The bride and groom requested that the guests avoid the colors burgundy, red, black and white since the bridal party would be wearing those.

"We are, and we're both stoked about it." Okay, maybe that was a slight exaggeration. They were doing each other a favor and keeping any prospective suitors away since neither wanted to be in a relationship.

Jade held up a lacy black dress, and Sienna wrinkled her nose before shaking her head.

"I don't like the big bow or belt on that empire waist." She knew the styles that would complement her best.

Jade returned it to the rack. "Just the use of the word 'stoked' has me suspicious. Are you two fighting?"

"A few differences of opinion can hardly be called *fighting*." Sienna wandered down the aisle. A colorful dress with a blend of pastel flowers caught her eye. It might do for the other wedding, where the bride had asked the guests to wear pink, blue or yellow with a hat.

Jade chuckled and followed behind. "Don't make it sound so civilized. I know you and Joel can't stand each other."

"We're learning to...communicate." She changed subjects. "Is Izzy still available to watch Micah while we're at the wedding?" Jade's daughter had just finished her junior year in high school and had gotten her first job at a boutique in the next town. The Three Amigas had banded together to purchase Izzy her first car, a used silver Honda Accord.

"Yes, and either Kelsey or I will be with Izzy, so

Micah will be in good hands," Jade said. "Now, quit trying to avoid my question. How are you and Joel going to pull this off without making a scene at the wedding?"

Sienna rolled her eyes. "We're adults. We won't be making any scenes."

"Excuse me, but weren't you two adults when you engaged in a shouting match at the church's garage sale? For the whole town to see?"

"That was three years ago. And that argument happened because the buffoon insisted on researching every single item before pricing. My way was quicker and more efficient, but he refused to admit that." Just remembering it now made Sienna's chest heave.

"His way brought in more funds."

She rolled her eyes again. "Whatever. But this time will be different. You'll see. Before, Pastor Reid had insisted on putting us to work the register together. He forced us to be partners. This time, we're doing this of our own free will." August Reid was the pastor of Millennial House of Praise, but had insisted they call him August since he was close to their ages. So far, Joel seemed to be the only one doing that with consistency.

"Hmmph."

Sienna plucked a dress off the rack and dangled it to examine the cut and details. Then she looked at the tag. "This should be a good fit."

"Wonderful." Jade ran her fingers through several hangers before holding up another dress. "How's this one?"

It was deep purple, with ruching and silver accents. "I like it."

"Perfect. Progress being made." Jade did a two-step in celebration.

Sienna lifted a hand, displaying her checkered nails. "Not so fast. I haven't tried them on—and if I can't find matching shoes, then it's a no go."

Jade heaved a sigh. "My smoothie isn't going to tide me over until lunch."

"Don't worry. I got you." Sienna dug into her bag and pulled out a honey-oat granola bar.

"Thank you, thank you." Jade slipped into one of the chairs, crossed her legs and gestured to Sienna to try on the dresses.

As Sienna had predicted, both dresses fit her full-figured frame perfectly, and she found shoes and bags to match. After visiting a couple more stores, Sienna found her other three dresses; then they drove back into Swallow's Creek to meet up with Kelsey for lunch. On the way, Sienna asked Jade to text Joel to bring Micah over for lunch. Her goddaughters were excited to meet the baby. And, though she had had fun shopping, Sienna missed Micah—his smile, his smell, his sounds—and couldn't wait to see him.

Sienna pulled into Kelsey's driveway, and Mia and Morgan came running out to greet them, wearing identical yellow summer dresses, with Jade's daughter, Izzy, running behind.

"Auntie Jade!" Morgan yelled.

"Aunt Sienna!" Mia squealed, her strap torn and her bun undone.

Sienna swallowed the emotions that always surfaced when she saw Morgan's happy face. She had been worried for her goddaughter after Morgan's adoptive parents had passed away in a car accident. But her aunt Kelsey had stepped up to care for her and then the twin sister no one knew Morgan had moved into town with Zach. The rest was history.

Both twins circled around Sienna. She bent over to give each a hug, then waggled her brows. "I see how you love your Auntie Sienna," she said to taunt Jade.

"Can we have chocolate?" Mia asked, bouncing around.

"Or candy?" Morgan asked, jumping.

Jade covered her mouth. "I knew there had to be something they wanted."

Sienna shrugged. She usually carried treats in her purse for them. Splaying her hands, she said, "I don't have anything today."

"Awww," Mia said.

Kelsey came to the door to announce that lunch was ready out back just as Joel was pulling up. Jade and Izzy headed around the house. Sienna scurried over to open the passenger door, only to see Micah's red face and hear him bellow.

One of the twins placed her hands over her ears. "He's loud."

Planting a hand on her hip, Sienna yelled at Joel, "What did you do to him?"

"Newsflash—he's a baby, and babies cry." Joel eased out his truck and stomped past Sienna with his jaw clenched. Not even five minutes, and she was calling him out in front of everyone. He knew his face was flushed red, because her words implied that he had harmed his nephew in some way. He reached for the diaper bag and swung it over his shoulders.

Sienna moved to take Micah out of his car seat and cradled him next to her. "Babies don't cry for no reason. He could be hungry..."

"I fed him," Joel snapped back.

"Or tired..."

"He just woke from a nap."

"Or needs changing."

"Did that too." He folded his arms and waited. Sienna's brows furrowed. Micah screamed and squirmed as if he was in pain.

Jade rushed back outside. "What's going on with Micah?"

Joel's heart pounded in his chest. "He started crying about an hour ago, and he won't stop."

"He might have gas." Jade held out a hand to take the baby from Sienna, who appeared to be on the verge of tears. She held the baby close and led them into Kelsey and Zach's home.

Somewhere in his mind, Joel registered the place as a lovely home, but besides spotting the house plant in the corner of the room, his mind was too focused on Micah to observe the space in detail. He did appreciate the cool blast from the central air, and he drew in deep breaths to keep from panicking.

"Do we need to call the doctor?" Joel asked, his stomach knotted. By this time, his nephew's lungs were operating at a pitch above natural level. He took a blanket out of the diaper bag and rested it on the couch.

Sienna hovered close to Joel. "Is he going to pass out?"

"Give me a minute, guys." Jade spoke in a calm tone before massaging Micah's tummy.

She ran her fingers in circular motion while Joel and

Sienna watched. In fact, Sienna surprised him when she took his hand. He clutched hers back, just as scared by the terror on Micah's face as she seemed to be.

Joel held his breath.

Sienna dabbed at her eyes. "I hope you know what you're doing, Jade."

A couple of tense minutes later, Micah let out a few burps, then a final howl before he hiccupped and yawned. Sienna dropped Joel's hand. He felt the loss but was happy to have feeling return to his fingers. Sienna had quite a grip.

Jade gently patted Micah's tummy. "There you go. You just needed a little help." Then she stood and wiped her hands on her jeans. After squeezing Joel's forearm, she left the room.

And Joel was alone with Sienna and Micah, who was now snoring contentedly on the couch.

She gave him a shy smile. "So apparently, every conversation we have has to be prefaced with an apology. So… I'm sorry if I embarrassed you in front of everyone."

He shoved his hands into his pockets. "I know I'm just as guilty as you are, but this arguing back and forth is getting tiring. Maybe you were right and I should get one of your students to watch him. One who won't question my every move or call me out in front of the entire neighborhood."

She touched his arm in the very same spot Jade had, but this time, a jolt went through his body. Her eyes were wide with panic. "No. I can do better. I know I'm not Micah's mom, but I love him." Her lips quivered. "Please allow me to keep watching him. I don't want to part with Micah until he's back home with his real mom."

He placed a hand on top of hers. Another shock, but he was determined to pretend like he felt nothing. "I understand you were scared, because I was too. I didn't know babies could cry like that." He gave her a pointed look. "But still… Don't do it again."

"I won't." She wrung her hands. "I promise."

With a nod, Joel let it go. Sienna excused herself while he took care of Micah's diaper. He knew Sienna had made a promise to do better, but he didn't know how long that would last. They were like fire and ice, oil and water—the real-life example of every kind of metaphor that existed to depict two things that should not go together.

Yet they both loved Micah, and maybe, just maybe, this infant would be the glue that kept them from tearing each other apart.

Chapter Eight

"Where are you going looking so fancy and sparkly?" Daphne asked on the evening of the first wedding, which took place on a Thursday. Sienna had her iPad mini perched on her chest of drawers so her mother could see her deep purple dress. It was loose and flowy, and Sienna felt like a princess.

She had gotten her braids redone in the front and styled in an updo, and had added hair jewelry. Instead of earrings, Sienna had chosen to wear a butterfly ear cuff over her right ear and a jeweled butterfly ring. Her nails were decorated with tiny rhinestones.

"One of my student teachers is getting married." She twirled around to give her mother a 360-degree view before asking, "You don't think it's too much? I have a mask that I have to wear during the reception."

"I think all that bling is all you, Sienna." Her mother wagged a finger. "I am sure you'll attract all the men at the wedding." Then she muttered, "Let's just hope they're single."

The slight disapproval in Daphne's voice gave Sienna pause. Picking up her iPad, Sienna made her way into the kitchen. She ran her hands down her dress, sat at the table and addressed her mother in a respectful manner, though on the inside, she was praying for patience. "I'm not dressing this way to snag a man, Mom. I dress for me. I earn a living to pay my bills but also to treat myself because I'm worth it, and I own that."

Her mother pinched the bridge of her nose. "I get that, but the wedding is about the bride. You don't want to attract all the attention, or you'll outshine the bride."

"Wow." Sienna counted to three and told herself to remain calm. "Mom, the theme of the wedding is *Phantom of the Opera*. We're supposed to be *fancy*, to use your word."

Sienna exhaled. She had called her mother to share her day—and yes, to hear her mother tell her that she looked good. Maybe get Daphne's stamp of approval. Somewhere inside her was that little girl who still refused to stop trying… Instead, Sienna felt disappointment squeeze her heart tighter than a kindergartner's pinch.

She clasped her hands on the table in front of her and lowered her chin. "Why couldn't you just tell me that I look beautiful? Why do you always try to deflate my confidence?" She dabbed at her eyes, furious with herself for expecting—for *wanting*—something that was as out of reach as a balloon filled with helium.

"That wasn't my intention." It was the genuine sadness in her mother's voice that made Sienna lift her head to look her mother in the eyes. Daphne gave her a sad smile. "As usual, I've made a mess of things. One day I'll get it right." She cleared her throat. "What I should have said was how stunning you are and how your smile is going to light up the room."

"Yes, I agree. That's what you should have said," she mumbled, her voice slightly bitter.

"I hate that I ruined a good conversation. Now things are awkward..." Daphne's brows furrowed, as if she was trying to think of something to say to break the tension.

Sienna was a grown woman who no longer needed validation on her worth or her beauty. She knew who she was even if no one else did, and that was more than enough.

Forcing a smile, Sienna felt her heart ease, converting it into a genuine one. "It's all good, Mom. I know you mean well," she breezed out. "I'm going to enjoy myself with my date tonight, and I'm going to eat a big slice of cake without an ounce of guilt."

"'Date'?" Daphne moved closer to the camera. "I thought you were going solo or with your Amigas."

Sienna chuckled. She knew mentioning that would revive the conversation. "Nope. I'm going with a dude."

"Oh." Daphne rubbed her hands together. "This is juicy. Who is he? What does he do?"

"He's a reporter. So please stop sending me pictures of all these random men, because I've got it handled."

Since their talk, Daphne had backed off on her matchmaking, and there had been no direct contact from any more men. But there had been photos that her mother had sent of the UPS driver, the supermarket manager and a man she met while on an afternoon walk. All of whom were interested in meeting the soon-to-be Dr. Sienna King. All of them received a thumbs-down emoji from Sienna.

She looked at her watch and then stood. “Now, I’ve got to get going because I’m sure he’s about to pull into the parking lot.”

“I can’t believe you held this bit of gossip until the end. I need details.”

“Bye, Mom.”

“Wait. Please say you’ll bring him by for dinner.”

“Let’s wait until I’m done with my dissertation.” Her mother’s rounded eyes when she pressed End made Sienna’s night. So when she got in Joel’s Jeep a few minutes later, she was in a good mood.

Her mother sent a text just as she closed the car door: I need proof. That made Sienna crack up. She sent her mother several question marks before turning to share the joke with Joel. But she noticed that he had the car in Park and was staring at her.

Her smile froze. “What’s wrong?”

“You… You look exquisite,” he sputtered. “I—I feel fortunate I get to say I’m with you.”

Now that was how you give a compliment! However, Joel made his living using words, so she shouldn’t let it go to her head.

Please. Who was she kidding? She was loving every second of his stupefied expression. Sienna giggled. “For once, I won’t argue with you. You *are* fortunate to be my date tonight.”

They shared a laugh before Joel drove out of the lot. And for the first time, she was looking forward to being in his company. “Here’s to having a good time tonight.”

A nail in the road had punctured their plans. Literally.

Joel had swerved onto the side of the road just before the tire blew out. Now he was manually pumping up the jack by the rear tire on a deserted road while Sienna alternated between tapping her feet and pacing. She had wanted to help once she realized he had never changed a tire before, but Joel had been set against it. There was no way he was going to risk her soiling or ripping that dress. He pulled up YouTube on his phone and followed the instructions step-by-step.

"I don't know why you find it hard accepting my help," Sienna said, pacing on the edge of the road. "I would have finished changing the flat and we would already be on our way if not for your stubbornness."

"I told you, I don't want you getting dirty," he huffed, taking off the lug nut and placing it on the ground. He would have, however, welcomed the assistance of another driver passing by. But so far, they had been the only ones on the road.

"All because you had to use the shortcut. The back road."

"It would have saved us time." Joel made a mental note to search online for a motorized tire jack. He was glad he had worn a black ensemble, but now he was so hot that he knew his shirt was going to have sweat stains.

"Well, it didn't." She rubbed her arms, her dress swaying in the evening breeze.

"Well, it could have."

"I don't want to be eaten alive by mosquitoes. So hurry up."

"I'm moving as fast as I can. The last thing I want is to be out here in the dark without streetlights." He loosened the other lug nut.

"We're not going to make the wedding."

"We will."

"I'm all dressed up with nowhere to go." She hummed a nondescript tune.

A muscle in his jaw twitched. "Your impatience isn't going to help this get done any faster."

"It's called *motivation*."

"More like maddening… bothersome… annoying."

Sienna flailed her hands and took out her cell phone. He presumed she was texting Kelsey and Jade to fill them in on their mishap, check on Micah, and, of course, complain about him. But it kept her quiet and distracted.

Finally, all the lug nuts were off. Joel jiggled the tire and removed it before standing to retrieve the spare and mount it. After that, the rest of the instructions were easy, and they were soon back inside the vehicle.

Sienna turned on the interior lights and studied her reflection. In his peripheral vision, he saw her reach into her small purse and pull out a small compact. Then she blotted her face with powder.

Sparing her a quick glance, he declared, "You look fine. You're going to dazzle the crowd."

"Correction: I look *more* than fine."

"I stand corrected." He saw her hand reach over his way and tilted his head away on pure instinct.

"You have a smudge on your face."

"Oh. I didn't know what you were going to do." He angled his head back toward her to give her easier access. Then her soft fingers touched his cheeks as she gave them a light rub. His breath hitched. The gesture felt couple-like and…intimate. He wondered if Sienna felt that way, too, but that was one question Joel knew he wouldn't ask. A new tension tightened his shoulders.

"There, I think I've got it." Her voice sounded soft, breathy. She felt the difference too; he was sure of it.

Joel gripped the wheel and told himself to act normal. But at the moment, he wasn't sure what that was. So he did what most people did when there was an awkward pause or lull in conversation: talked about the weather. "I'm so glad it didn't rain today. Because changing a tire wouldn't have been fun."

She seemed to grab on to the topic with gusto. "Yes, it is the perfect weather for an evening wedding. You did a great job with the tire, by the way."

"Stop the presses. Is Sienna King acknowledging that I did something right?"

"Well, the vehicle is still upright and moving, so I suppose I am."

Joel cracked up, relaxing his shoulders. "I need to record the day and time because history has been made."

"I can't with you." Sienna snorted. It was unladylike and sounded like a honk, but it made Joel smile. Usually, when she said those words, they were filled with disgust or agitation. Today, they'd been delivered in jest—kind of like how you would banter with a friend. He found that he liked it. He liked it a lot.

Chapter Nine

The aisle was lined with a red carpet and the altar surrounded by large decorative roses. There were round tables with black chairs and red trimmings and large candelabras as centerpieces. Each seat had golden plates and champagne glasses wrapped with pearls. The cake was black, white and red, and sported a phantom's mask on the side.

The only thing missing was the bride.

Sienna stood by the entrance, her eyes wide, her mouth open—not at the majestic scene but at the fact that the space was empty. All the guests were outside, milling around, whispering about the potential no-show bride.

The groom, Montel, stood surrounded by his circle of friends. His shirt was undone, and he was gesturing wildly with his hands. Since he happened to be Joel's former coworker, Joel left Sienna's side to join the huddle and, she suspected, get the 411 on what was truly going on.

Sienna made eye contact with another guest, who took that as an invitation to sidle up next to her. The woman was dressed in a cream linen pantsuit. Her eyes sparkled like she had been waiting for someone to gossip with about the night's non-events.

"Friend of the groom?" Without waiting for an answer, the woman continued, "I heard the bride is suffering from a serious case of cold feet."

"Really?" Her brows rose. The bride, Fatima, was actually one of Sienna's former mentees. She had been Fatima's mentor teacher, and Sienna had given Fatima a great recommendation for the teacher position. "I'm surprised to hear that, because she was really excited about marrying Montel. In fact, that was all she talked about for months."

"Right before you came, her husband-to-be announced that we shouldn't leave. He's determined to wait. That woman doesn't deserve him." It was her scathing tone that really triggered Sienna's ire.

"How do you know that?"

The woman shrugged. "You just never know… People are shady. I hear she might have run off with someone from work." She covered her mouth with her hand to hide a giggle, clearly expecting Sienna would join in.

Sienna folded her arms. "I'm not about to judge anybody without getting the facts, and I don't think it's right to assume the worst when we don't know what happened." The Fatima Sienna knew wouldn't leave the groom at the altar like that without good reason.

"I… I wouldn't do that," the woman sputtered, her face red.

"Do you have a job?" Sienna shot out.

"Yes. Why? What does that have to do with anything?"

"Mind the business you get paid for, and keep it moving."

The woman's mouth dropped open, and she clutched her chest. "I was just making conversation. You don't have to be insulting."

Sienna swirled her index finger. "Keep that nonsense to yourself. I'm not the one to entertain speculation. As the saying goes, assumptions and presumptions are not my friends."

Without uttering another word, the woman stalked over to join a group of young ladies. All Sienna could do was shake her head. She had tried to reach Fatima, but she hadn't received a response, which was no surprise. Fatima must be bombarded with texts and calls. Still, she did send Fatima a text, asking her to reach out if she needed help. She hoped Fatima and Montel would get to recite their vows tonight, because those two loved each other. He was a fixture at their school, and they clung to each other like syrup on sticky buns. Sienna might not believe in love for herself, but she rooted for happy-ever-afters for others.

"I see I'm not the only one who has gotten a tongue-lashing," Joel said from behind her.

She spun around. "Where did you come from? Did you hear all that?"

He chuckled. "Yes."

Sienna groaned. "I was probably too harsh, but she was making snide remarks against Fatima, which wasn't cool. I had to check her."

"Well, I would say you schooled her well." He laughed. "I came over to see if you wanted water and if you happened to have heard from Fatima."

"No. I don't need anything to drink. I'm good. And as for Fatima, I reached out, but I doubt she'll call me." On cue, her phone rang. Sienna's mouth popped open. She held up the cell phone so Joel could see. "It's Fatima."

Joel's eyes practically bulged, and then he gestured by waving a hand. "Answer, answer!"

"Hey, Fatima… Are you okay?" Sienna kept her tone neutral and open, though her insides were shaky.

"Hey…" The other woman sounded hesitant, her voice hoarse like she had been crying. "I know everyone must be wondering where I am, but I don't know what to do, and when I saw your text, I decided to call."

Sienna touched her chest. "I'm glad you felt safe to call me." She could hear the torture and indecision in Fatima's voice, and she didn't want to say the wrong thing and scare her off. "Where are you? Do you need me to come see you?"

"Y-yes. I was there, but then I hijacked one of the bridesmaids' cars and left." Fatima disclosed her location, which was only five minutes away.

"Stay where you are. I'm coming." Sienna tossed her phone into her purse and began to run. "We've got to get to her before she gets spooked and leaves." Sienna's heart pounded.

Joel took her hand, and they raced across the grass to his Jeep. One good thing about arriving late was that they were parked close to the exit. Three minutes later due to Joel's speeding, they were pulling into the abandoned storage building. They drove to the back.

Sure enough, Fatima stood outside the vehicle. The hemline of her couture gown had a ring of dirt and grass that Sienna was sure would become a permanent stain. Fatima's eyes were wide with fright and her makeup had been ruined from tears. She had a serious case of raccoon eyes, and her cheeks were splotchy.

Following her instincts, Sienna rushed over and grabbed the younger woman in a hug. Joel stayed by the Jeep, but he was still within earshot.

"I c-can't marry Montel." Fatima fell apart in her arms. Her shoulders shook, and Sienna could feel as her own gown got soaked from the tears.

After letting Fatima release some of the tension, Sienna pulled away. She gently moved Fatima's curls, frizzy and ruined by the humidity, out of her face. "Can you tell me what's wrong?"

"I…" Fatima lolled her head back, overcome with grief. She wrung her hands. To Sienna, Fatima seemed like she wanted to talk but was just too overwhelmed to speak.

"Take deep breaths."

Fatima complied.

Joel cleared his throat. "I'll be back. I'm going to give you two a few minutes to talk."

Sienna gave Joel a grateful smile. She thought his leaving was thoughtful and wise. Sure enough, once he was gone, Fatima spilled like water from a faucet.

"I found out I have a tumor." Her lips quivered.

Sienna gasped, covering her mouth. It took a lot, but she remained silent and gestured so that Fatima could keep speaking.

"I went to get a routine checkup and just happened to mention that I was suffering from headaches, and the doctor recommended a CT scan." Her hands flailed. "Then, voilà."

Sienna curled her fingers around Fatima's arm. "I'm

so sorry to hear this. What did Montel say when you told him?"

"He doesn't know." She wrung her hands some more. "I just got the call earlier today, right as the wedding procession began. That's when I bolted."

Sienna's brows furrowed. "You were taking your cell phone with you down the aisle?"

Patting her gown, Fatima said, "It has pockets." She drew in a shaky breath. "A part of me wishes I had never answered. I would be married and clueless right now. But I'm probably dying, and I can't put Montel through that."

"I understand you're scared and panicked, but leaving him at the altar isn't the way to go." She saw Fatima's eyes go wide. "Montel is distraught, but he is there, waiting. For you. And he told everybody not to leave. That's how sure he is about you. Listen, I'm the first to tell you that I'm not looking for love, but if I were, I would want a man who looks at me the way Montel does you."

"He does like to stare at me sometimes." Fatima lowered her head. "I don't think he'll want to see me after this stunt today though. He must be furious."

"I don't think he's furious, but I do know that he's waiting."

Joel's Jeep swerved around the corner, and he came to a neat stop. He jumped out of his vehicle, and Sienna stepped back in shock when she saw Montel get out right after him. When Fatima saw him, she hurled herself into Montel's arms.

Joel and Sienna leaned against his Jeep while Fatima and Montel kissed. Both he and Sienna had tried to remind them that they had guests waiting and a wedding to attend, but neither Fatima nor Montel had budged. Joel shifted and looked away from their open display of affection—of love—fighting against the surprising jealousy settling in his chest.

Fatima had divulged her news and given Montel an out, but Montel made it known that even if he had one day left with her, they would spend it as husband and wife. Then he recited his vows. Now, Joel wasn't a romantic, but that had been a scene fit for any romance book. Sienna had dabbed at her eyes while Joel blinked back a sudden onslaught of emotions. He'd wondered what it was like to be so certain about a woman. The one woman he had thought would be by his side for life had run off before his wedding. Just like Montel. Only Montel's bride had done it out of fear, not bribery. And Montel's bride loved him.

"That was a smart move," Sienna said, nudging his arm and bringing him out of his thoughts. "You were the hero of the night, getting Montel here. All she had to do was see his face, and that settled her like nothing else."

Joel thought he heard a slight longing in her voice, but he knew better than to ask. Instead, he focused on responding to her comment.

"Thanks. When I went over to talk with him, Montel kept saying that he just needed to see her. When I told him I knew where she was, I promise you that I have never seen a big man move that fast." Montel was built like a defensive football player. He'd been playing for the NFL when an injury ended his career, so he had taken up journalism. Both Joel and Montel had attended school together. "I wish I had recorded that."

"Hey, you two. Knock it off." Sienna leaned across

him, and he caught a powdery scent. She yelled in her teacher voice, "We've got to get back to *your* wedding."

The couple ended their kiss, and after a quick apology, Sienna repaired Fatima's makeup as best as she could. With a quick word of thanks, Montel jumped into the car with Fatima and took off. Joel and Sienna did the same. During the drive, Sienna kept her attention on her phone. He returned to the same parking spot, and once he turned off the engine, Sienna placed her phone on her lap and touched his arm.

"I hope today wasn't hard for you."

He gave her a quizzical look. "What do you mean?"

"Well, this was almost a repeat of what you went through, only it had a happier outcome." She lowered her head and clasped her hands in her lap.

"I was just thinking about that a few minutes ago and yes, I'm so relieved that Montel's day is ending way differently than mine did all those years ago." He smiled. "It felt good to see him happy and in love."

He could hear the strains of the bridal procession, but after all the events of the evening, Joel wasn't worried about missing the main event. As far as he was concerned, the real wedding had taken place outside the storage building.

"Do you still…?" Sienna trailed off and looked outside.

Somehow Joel knew she was asking if he still had feelings for his ex. He turned on the interior lights of the Jeep. "If I'm being honest, I wasn't the wreck like Montel was tonight. I was upset and humiliated, but my heart was all right. I won't make that same mistake again, though."

She turned to face him. "Do you think you'd ever want to have a family one day?"

Unexpectedly, an image of Sienna and Micah hit his mind. But he ignored it and said, "I don't think it will happen for me. But I'm content with spoiling Micah." He laughed. "I plan to be the uncle who gives him crazy gifts, like a moped at ten years old or something."

They shared a laugh. "What about you?"

"I'd like to have a child of my own." She folded her arms around herself. "Taking care of Micah is so rewarding. Every day, he gives me a reason to smile." Her face glowed under the lights, and Joel felt mesmerized by her beauty before he caught himself. What on earth was he doing? He and Sienna might be getting on well tonight, but he couldn't forget that it was because they both loved Micah. Once Micah was gone, their truce would be over and they would be back to being frenemies.

So he changed the subject. "I'd better text Kelsey and Jade and let them know that we're going to be late getting back."

"Already on it. I texted them on the ride over. They even sent a picture." She tapped on her phone and pulled up a photo of Micah dressed in a onesie with an elephant on it. His eyes were closed, and his little hands were fisted by each of his ears.

"Isn't he the cutest?" Sienna cooed. "I could stare at him all day."

And I could stare at her *all day.* The realization struck Joel in the gut. He grabbed the handle and opened the door. Air. He drew in a deep breath and hopped out, relieved to exit the cozy confines of his vehicle. It was messing with his head. Then he opened Sienna's door, helped her out and extended his arm. "Let's go enjoy that wedding."

She looped her arm through his. Because of her height and those heels, they were a good fit. A right fit. His stomach muscles tightened. The notion of that was…ridiculous. Preposterous. Some day he would laugh his head off about it.

But today wasn't that day.

Chapter Ten

"It wasn't the words that he spoke," Sienna said to Jade the next morning. "It was the way he said it, like he was truly in love." Jade had stopped by Joel's house the next morning, with apple muffins, to talk about the wedding. They were sitting side by side on the couch, and Sienna had just filled her in on the ceremony that almost hadn't happened and Montel's display of affection.

Micah was upstairs in the nursery, and she had the baby monitor on the coffee table in front of her.

"I'm so glad you and Joel were able to reunite them." Jade touched her chest. Her hand covered the *Too Blessed* portion of the "Too Blessed to Be Stressed" written on the orange shirt she had tucked into her white shorts.

"It was so romantic. There wasn't a dry eye in the house when they shared their wedding dance. Then, to top off the night, Montel surprised her with a honeymoon trip to Italy."

"Aw. How sweet. Makes me almost want a husband of my own." Then she scoffed and rolled her eyes. "As if. I'd rather pull both my front teeth than get married again."

Right at that moment, Sienna's mother called on FaceTime. She answered, surprised to see both her parents sitting next to each other. Daphne touched her scarf and played with it. Her face was puffy and her eyes red—a sign that she had been crying. The only time Sienna ever remembered her mother crying was at Sage's funeral.

Deep in her gut, Sienna knew that meant her mother didn't have good news. Sienna grew somber, her hands shaking. Jade greeted Sienna's parents before saying she would go.

"No, Jade," Daphne called out. "Please… Stay. I'm glad you're there."

With a nod, Jade returned to Sienna's side. Sienna gripped her hand.

Daphne and Lennox joined hands, and then her mother squared her shoulders. "I—I don't know how to say this, Sienna, so I might as well just blurt it out. I'm—I'm dying."

Jade gasped.

Sienna lost her breath for a second. "Wh-What do you mean you're *dying*? You've never been sick a day in your life. In fact, when I got chicken pox, you took care of me even though you never had it yourself."

"Sienna."

Her mother spoke her name with such finality that it stilled her ramblings. Sienna massaged her temples; Jade rubbed her back. "I don't believe you."

Lennox chimed in. "It's true. We had two physicians confirm it. Your mother has stage four liver cancer, and it's inoperable."

Sienna's brows furrowed. "How? You never drank a day in your life."

"The iron in my system caused a buildup, which led to cirrhosis and then liver…cancer."

The certainty with which her mother spoke settled in her core like bricks. Tears sprang to Sienna's eyes. Her body shook under the impact of the revelation. "This can't be happening. It can't be true." Her heart felt sliced and ravaged. She leaned into Jade's shoulder and sobbed, her tears filled with regret, fear and sorrow.

"The doctors are predicting that I have between six to eleven months." Her mother dabbed at her eyes, but Sienna knew Daphne wasn't about to fall apart. No matter what happened in her life, Daphne remained composed. Except for when it came to Sage.

She gasped. "I'm leaving today."

Her mother held up a hand. "No. I need time to process everything. Besides, I really need you to finish prepping for your dissertation."

Sienna addressed her father. "Please tell me you don't agree with her."

"I just want your mother happy."

Her shoulders slumped. She should have known her father would take her mother's side. "Mom, you tell me you've got months…" Her voice cracked. "Months to live, and you want me to keep working on my doctorate? Are you listening to yourself right now?"

"First, don't get disrespectful. I'm still your mother."

"I'm sorry, Mom."

Daphne gave a regal nod. "Now, to answer your question, Sienna. Yes, that's what I want." Her face crumpled. "I'm the one who's sick, not you. You don't get to decide what I do with the time I have left."

"I can't bear the thought of losing you," Sienna whispered. She couldn't fathom not having her mother in her life. Not seeing her or hearing her voice, even if her face was filled with disapproval and her words with disappointment—Sienna realized that didn't matter as much. Her mother was here. And soon, she wouldn't be.

"This is God's business," her mother said. "We don't get to decide."

Her parents hung up after that. Sienna turned to her friend and gave a sad chuckle. "Now my mom will be more determined to set me up with a man. See me settled before she..."

No. Her mother couldn't be dying. She was too young, too vibrant.

Jade shook her head. "She's one of the fittest and healthiest people I know. I don't get it."

"I'm floored as well." Sienna lifted her shoulders. "But you see how she's adamant that I don't go up there."

Jade's eyes held sympathy. "I think this may be a case where her your mother's mouth is saying one thing, but her heart is saying another."

She tilted her head. "You think so?"

"I'm a mom. I know so." Jade patted her hand. "I think you need to go see her. She might fuss, but in her heart, she will be glad to have you there."

"I don't know... Me and my mother have never had the kind of relationship you see in the movies. We don't confide in each other. We've never hung out or got our hair done together. Everything with us was and still is a tug-of-war." She bit her lower lip. "The last thing I want is to show up and somehow enrage my sick mother."

Jade placed a hand across her chest. "As a mother, my heart breaks to see you so uncertain. No child should be unsure about their position with their parent, or in your case, parents. Frankly, that's the one relationship that you should be able to take for granted. You should know that they are always going to support you no matter what you do. Because you know that they love you and they are in your corner."

Tears filled Sienna's eyes. "I didn't have that security growing up," she whispered. "I still don't… And I don't get it. Micah isn't my biological child, but I know I love him. I know I want the best for him, and I know I would do everything in my power to protect him. And it's only been a couple weeks since he's been in my life." She squared her shoulders. "Meanwhile, I've been with my parents a lifetime, and I know my parents love me—I just don't always feel it." She met Jade's gaze. "I know it makes no sense, but I really believe that if I don't get this doctorate degree, they are going to love me a little less. And now my mom wants me to find a husband…"

Jade gripped both Sienna's arms and gave her a light shake. "You don't have to earn their love. It should be freely given. Just the way God loves us. Take that weight off your shoulders. Listen, Kelsey and I are already proud of you, without those letters behind your name. If the degree is what you want, keep going until you get it, but stop putting pressure on yourself. You act like you're in a race—but, honey, you're the only one running. So you know what that means?" Jade relaxed her grip, paused and arched a brow. Sienna shook her head. "Since you're the only contestant, it means you can take all the time you want and need to cross that finish line."

Relief seeped through Sienna's body at those words, and she exhaled. "You're so right."

Jade patted Sienna's shoulder. "And if Kelsey was here, she would say the same thing."

"Has her nausea eased up any?"

"No, but she's already wondering if she can still compete in this year's Sports Day events at our church picnic."

Sienna laughed, picturing her very pregnant friend trying to do the potato-sack or three-legged race. Every year, the church hosted a sports day on the Fourth of July. "Kelsey will have to sit out this summer. I'm sure Zach told her not to even try."

"I agree. I think she was kidding around, but you know she's thinking about that trophy."

Every year before her sister Kennedy's death, Kelsey and Kennedy had been the reigning champs. Then Zach had filled that vacant spot so Kelsey could maintain her number one position. She had a fierce competitive spirit.

"Well, she can root for her twins from the sidelines."

"Are you still on the committee?"

Jade nodded. "I'll be working with Pastor Reid to organize the event. We're thinking of doing a carnival this year. I don't know how I'm going to manage all that and start up a business, but he talked me into it." Sienna wasn't surprised; Pastor Reid could be very convincing. Jade gave her a speculative glance. "You know he's meeting with Joel this morning."

"Yes, he told me..." She kept her expression and tone neutral. Anytime either of her friends mentioned Joel, they gave her a certain look. Like they wanted to see how she would react. But Sienna pretended like she hadn't noticed.

"He's planning to ask Joel to be a judge at the carnival. Speaking of which—I know you're busy, but I hope you'll also think about judging. Zach's already agreed."

"I'll let you know." Sienna changed the subject. "How's the launch going?" With everything that was going on, she hadn't been over to see how Jade's personal gym was coming along.

Jade ran her hands through her pixie cut. "Ugh. It's been one thing after another, but I'm not deferring this dream anymore." Her voice held determination. "Compared to single motherhood, this is a breeze."

"If anyone can juggle it all and make it look easy, I know you can."

A little whimper came through the monitor, and Sienna sprang to her feet. "It looks like I'm back on duty." She rushed to warm up his bottle, knowing his whimpers could quickly escalate to wails in a short time.

Jade also stood. "That sounds like my exit cue." She blew Sienna an air-kiss and bounded toward the front door. "We'll catch up soon. Let me know what you decide to do about visiting your mother."

"Skip, I thought when you gave me this promotion that you said I wouldn't have to travel as much or do any more fluff pieces." Joel stood across from the large oak desk in his boss's office. It was a corner office, and aside from a couch, several armchairs and a couple of potted plants, Skip kept the space sparse.

He didn't know why Skip had turned his desk away

from the magnificence of the water behind him. If Joel was in here, he would be constantly distracted by the incredible view. Today the sky was a clear blue, and there wasn't a cloud in sight. Remarkable. Breathtaking. Hmm… Maybe that's why Skip's desk had been turned away. Skip had his head down as he studied the print run of the next-day's paper. Though most of their readers read the paper online, Swallow's Creek had a large audience that still wanted the print edition.

His boss looked up and waved a liver-spotted, gnarled hand in Joel's direction. "Yes, but one of Swallow's Creek High's seniors has been drafted to the NFL. The Pittsburgh Steelers. It was in the seventeenth round, but it's still big news."

"I agree. I've followed Jayvaughn Trevor since he was knee-high, but this is a gig for one of the junior editors, not for me. I'm still working the fire at Mr. MacGrady's. The cops believe they're close to catching the perp who did this."

Skip dug into his pocket and pulled out two mints. He tore open the personalized wrapping and then popped one in his mouth.

"I get that you think this assignment is beneath you. But the media attention on this young man is big. He's the fourth in his family to get drafted. The fourth. That's epic. Unheard of. So you need to pack a bag and get out there for his arrival at the NFL rookie minicamp on Monday."

"I…can't." Joel lifted his khaki-colored baseball cap off his head and adjusted his yellow T-shirt over his jeans.

Skip's eyes narrowed, and he pinned Joel with a fierce glare. "*Can't* or *won't*?"

"I've got a child. My nephew is staying with me."

"You told me that. You also told me it wouldn't interfere with your job."

"It hasn't. But going to Pittsburgh would mean I have to spend the night. I have Micah to think of now."

Skip arched a brow and pointed toward the exit. "Lucky was my first consideration for the associate editor position because he's been here the longest, and he has as much accolades as you do. But he has a family, and he said he wouldn't commit to leaving his wife and children for extended periods of time. That's why I chose you. You're single, unattached, and I don't even think you're dating."

"That can't be the main reason you hired me. That goes against our employment practices."

"Of course that's not the only reason. You're talented and nationally recognized. But availability is a part of the job description. I offered the job to Lucky, and he turned it down."

The knowledge that he had been second choice soured Joel's stomach before he steeled himself. Tom Brady and Joe Montana hadn't made round one or two drafts, yet they were legendary football players. He would be the same.

He squared his shoulders. "I'll be there by Monday."

"Good. That's what I want to hear. Phillipa will set up your accommodations," Skip said, speaking with finality. Joel knew that was his cue to leave.

He trudged into his own office and closed the door. Sinking into his chair, he placed his head in his hands. His eyes landed on Micah's photo, and guilt lined his stomach at the thought of leaving him. But he reminded himself that he had a job to do that helped him to provide the care that Micah needed.

Joel prayed Sienna would be okay with keeping Micah for a couple of days. At the same time, he felt a pang—he was going to miss the little guy. Joel looked forward to seeing him at the end of the day. He would rest him on his blanket and play with him. That time with his nephew had become the highlight of his evenings. He knew he was on borrowed time; Micah would be reunited with his parents soon. Joel just didn't know how he would have the strength to let him go when the time came.

He sighed and rubbed his eyes. Might as well text Sienna to ask her about keeping Micah and get that potential unpleasant task out of the way. Hey...are you able to keep Micah for a couple days? Three at the most.

What's going on? she texted back almost immediately.

I have to go to Pittsburgh from Sunday to Tuesday.

He watched the dots dance, and his stomach knotted as waited for her response.

The mayor's daughter's wedding is Sunday.

That's right. He'd almost forgot about that. His fingers flew over the keyboard. I would leave after that.

Okay. I'll do it. But on one condition...

He waited a few seconds before he typed, What???

Take me with you.

Chapter Eleven

"We can't forget to pose together for a photo at this wedding, since we didn't at the last one. I need to show my mother that I'm really in a relationship so that she will stop trying to set me up with these random men," Sienna reminded Joel when they pulled up into the parking lot of the wedding venue at about 1:00 p.m. that Sunday.

Sienna hopped out of the Jeep and frowned. She could already smell the hay bales and hear pigs squealing in one of the buildings. The couple had chosen to have their wedding on a farm. She was glad the actual wedding would take place under a large tent instead of inside the barn.

"Consider it done." He gave her a side glance before sweeping his eyes over her pastel-print dress.

Sienna had donned buttercup-yellow shoes and a wide-brimmed yellow straw hat. She had chosen chunky pink and blue jewelry and pinned her braids into a bun. But the masterpiece was her matching pastel nails. She had waited until that morning to get them done and was pleased with the results. When Joel saw her, he had eyed her with appreciation.

He wore a light blue shirt with navy blue slacks and dress shoes. Sienna had given him a once-over and declared that they would go shopping for a suit before the third wedding. She couldn't keep flexing with Joel by her side if he wasn't going to bring it.

He came around to open the door for her. She stepped out, holding on to the hat brim to keep it from falling off her head.

Joel reached into the back seat to retrieve his camera. The bride was the mayor's daughter, Marisa, and most of the press had been banned from attending. But somehow, Joel had convinced Marisa to let him take a few pictures and do a special piece from the groom's perspective. One way or another, Joel would get his story.

"How's your mother doing?"

Sienna cleared her throat. "I'll find out when I see her tomorrow. She doesn't know I plan to visit or that I'll be going to Pittsburgh with you. Maybe she could meet you in person…?" Her heart pounded while Joel stood silently, like he was in deep thought.

After she had responded to his text, asking him to take her with him, Sienna had been all smiles when he responded with a quick yes. She accounted for her better mood because she was going to see her mother in person. Then she called the nearest hotel to reserve two rooms.

"Since we'll be getting there late tonight, I can meet your mother after I'm done with my interview with Jayvaughn." When Joel had gotten in from work that evening, he told her all about his assignment in Pittsburgh.

Joel had been almost remorseful for putting her out of her way until she filled him in on her reason for going with him. Like Jade, he'd thought it was a good idea for her to visit her mom, and he hadn't tried to hide his joy that he wouldn't be away from Micah for two nights.

They had dropped Micah off at Jade's and would pick him up after the wedding, then be on their way. Sienna and Joel had already packed the rear of Jeep and it was at capacity. Nothing else could fit back there. They both had been surprised at how much was needed to travel with an infant—not to mention Sienna had packed a large suitcase for herself as well. For only a two-day trip. They had had a brief spat about it, but she'd been insistent that she would need everything inside. Joel, on the other hand, only had a large backpack, which had been met with a dubious stare.

Joel retrieved his wedding gift from the car, cradling it under his arm. Sienna had mailed hers in advance, not wanting to worry about toting anything but her fine self to the wedding.

"Your mom might think you're joking when she sees it's me," he teased her. "She might remember me."

"There's a bigger chance that she won't. My parents are focused. Driven. They don't take time to smell the roses… Or rather, they didn't used to."

Sienna was glad she had worn wedges, because walking on the grass to the tent would have ruined the heels of her pumps.

"Speaking of smells, I think my allergies are acting up." Joel suddenly sneezed several times in succession.

Patting her purse, Sienna said, "I have some vitamin

C tablets in a Ziploc bag. I'll give you some once we're under the tent."

"You walk around with vitamins in your purse?" he asked in amazement.

"Yep. A habit from being an educator all these years and going on all those field trips. I have to be prepared."

"Doesn't vitamin C help with colds?"

"Yes, but I have used it to counteract an allergic reaction I had to Swai fish and it helped big time."

He stopped for a beat and stilled her by touching her arm. "You are remarkable, Sienna King. Simply remarkable."

She arched a brow, trying to think of a snarky comeback that would cover the fact that she felt delight at his compliment on the inside. But her brain wouldn't cooperate. Maybe because she was too busy taking in the earnest expression on his face. So she simply said, "Thank you," and kept walking. It occurred to her then that they had gone a whole car ride without arguing, and she smiled.

"What's that smile about?" he asked, walking in step with her.

"It's nothing."

"What is it?"

She was saved from answering by the fact that they'd reached the edge of the tent. In keeping with the theme, the tables were covered with burlap and decorated in pastels, mostly pink, blue and yellow. It looked classy and whimsical at the same time. A live band was set up on the makeshift stage, plus there was a deejay. There were massive amounts of flowers of all kinds, which filled the air with pleasant smells and almost helped you forget you were on a farm. Almost.

"Hmmph."

"What's that *hmmph* for?" she demanded, placing a hand on her hip.

"I just thought we were at the point where we could share what's on our minds, that's all." He seemed to be put out by her, and that fired up her temper.

"This is unbelievable," Sienna fumed, muttering so that only he could hear since other guests were approaching. "All I was thinking was that we weren't arguing and it felt nice, and you had to go ruin it."

His mouth popped open. "Oh. Now I feel dumb."

"I won't argue with that." She stomped over to find their name cards since it was open seating while Joel went to place his gift on the designated table. Getting a whiff of his cologne, she turned to him.

"I'm sorry."

Her chest heaved. "It wasn't a big deal, which is why I told you I didn't want to say anything."

He stood watching her for a moment before his lips quirked, and he snickered. Soon his shoulders were shaking.

"What's so funny?" she asked, debating whether to bop him on the head or grab a seat without him.

"It's just that we're arguing about not arguing. That's new for us." He laughed loud enough to draw attention.

Laughter bubbled within her, and she ended up joining in. Their laughter washed away her ire, and it took a minute before she settled. She gave him a light jab. "You're going to make me ruin my makeup. The last thing I want is to look like a raccoon and scare off the bride."

"That would be impossible. You're beautiful." He spoke with such calm certainty that Sienna had to look away as a sudden shyness overtook her.

Then she scolded herself. This was Joel, so she had better not read more into his words. In fact, she should be worried about the compliment. He could be setting her up for a laugh. She cleared her throat and fished around in her purse for her pocket mirror. "The mirror tells the truth, and I wouldn't put it past you to have me walking around looking like a hot mess." She peered into the small oval glass and saw that all was well. Just as he had said.

"You see? Beautiful."

This time, she simply thanked him and led the way for them to choose their seats. She wanted to be in the far corner, out of the spotlight, but Joel picked a spot closer to the action. He admitted that he needed to capture some good pictures of the bride and groom. So that's how she ended up with an almost-front-row view of the festivities. Sienna retrieved the vitamin C pills from her bag for her and Joel. She handed one to him, and she took the other.

"I forgot to ask how you got an invitation to the wedding," Joel said, then popped the pill in his mouth and sipped his water. "It's a pretty swanky affair."

"I tutored the mayor's son, plus his daughter and I were friends in college."

"Oh, I see." He tapped the table, his legs moving to the beat of the music the deejay was playing. "My boss snagged me an invite when he assigned this story, or

I doubt that I would have been among the chosen few who got to attend."

"I thought you were in charge of choosing the stories and assignments now," she said.

"I am, but Skip still has the ultimate say-so and the authority to send me out on special projects. Like this one and the one in Pittsburgh."

Sienna reached into her purse to get a pen to make her food selection for dinner. The choice was between filet mignon, chicken cacciatore or garlic-butter salmon. She circled the garlic-butter salmon and then gave Joel the pen. With a bold swoop of the pen, he went for the filet mignon.

Looking up at her, he shrugged. "Why not?" Their eyes connected.

His hair fell into his face, and that was when her breath caught. Joel Armstrong was one handsome man. She fanned herself, wondering how she hadn't noticed before that all his features blended well together. Like, really well.

She watched his eyes narrow like he was about to ask why she was staring, but fortunately, his cell phone rang. A welcomed interruption. "Hold that thought," he said, answering the phone as he walked toward the edge of the tent. The music was pretty loud.

Sienna slumped against her chair and berated herself for her lapse in judgment. She had just drooled over Joel—the annoying, aggravating kid from second grade. Maybe it was the lighting in the tent or the flowers making her dizzy, because that wouldn't happen again. She couldn't get caught up in their pretense when she wasn't interested in dating anyone. And even if she was, it certainly wouldn't be Joel. Right?

His phone had a way of ringing during the most inopportune times. If it were anybody besides his brother, his boss or Jade, Joel would have ignored it. He wanted to know what that look Sienna had given him was about. But it was Greg, so he took the call, his stomach muscles tense.

"Hey there, how's Tessa?" He held his breath while he waited for Greg's answer, praying and hoping it wasn't bad news.

"She's awake! She's awake!" Greg yelled, his voice filled with excitement. "Tessa opened her eyes about an hour ago."

Joel pumped his fists. "Yes. Bro, I'm so excited for you. This is wonderful." He paced the outside of the tent.

"Yes, as soon as she is able, they will begin therapy. And if everything goes according to plan, Tessa should be home in a few weeks."

That meant his time with Micah was coming to an end soon. He felt a pang, already knowing he was going to miss the little guy. "I know Tessa must be asking for Micah."

"Those were her first words—'How's Micah?' She broke down when I told her that Micah was in another state. I feel so guilty for sending him with you so far away."

"You did what you thought was best. Micah is with family. I hope you told her that I am doing all I can for him and I am loving having him here with me."

Greg's face softened. "Yes, I did tell her that. She's

happy to hear that we've reunited and that you're helping out with Micah. But we miss our baby boy." His voice broke.

Joel swallowed. "I understand." Now guilt washed over him. Maybe he should have taken time off and stayed close. Maybe coming back to Swallow's Creek was a sign of his selfishness. Because his brother sounded tortured, and Joel didn't want to even begin thinking about how Tessa must feel.

"It's not that I'm not grateful… It's that…" His brother trailed off, sounding uncertain.

He heard the deejay announce that the wedding would begin soon. He knew he had to go talk with the mayor or the groom. Joel cupped the phone to his ear and began to walk back inside. "How about I FaceTime you both later so she can see Micah? I'm at a wedding right now, and I have to take photos. But I promise to call as soon as I am home."

"Yeah, cool. I'd like that… Thanks, bro."

"All right, see you then." Walking back to his table, Joel reflected on his brother and wife being separated from their only child. Joel could hear the longing in his brother's voice. He didn't know how Greg was able to handle being without Micah for this long. Joel had been away from his nephew for only an hour, and he was missing him with a fierceness he didn't know possible. Joel was so attached; he knew he would have a hard time letting him go. And that time seemed closer than he thought.

Chapter Twelve

The deejay announced that the bridal party was about to enter, and Sienna forgot all about her embarrassing moment with Joel. Perched at the edge of the chair, she almost gasped when she saw the bride was wearing pink. It was tasteful, elegant—formfitting on top and a flowing skirt with yards and yards of tulle at the bottom. Marisa had the attitude to pull off that daring look.

Sienna grabbed her cell and took several pictures to post in the Amigas group chat. Her description of the dress wouldn't do it justice.

Marisa's headpiece consisted of a pearl crown and silver veil that extended about a hundred feet, embroidered with pink, yellow and blue chrysanthemums. The groom, Tucker, wore a baby blue suit and light pink shirt. His shoes and corsage were a dusty yellow. Sienna didn't know how the stylist had pulled it off, but Tucker looked sharp, giving off movie-star vibes.

The wedding party's outfits were the distraction Sienna needed to keep her focus off the man standing a few feet away from her, snapping pictures next to the videographers and professional photographers.

Sienna and the other guests *ooh*ed and *aah*ed when the ring bearer and flower girl headed down the aisle; they were too cute for words. Then Marisa headed toward her groom, and Tucker broke into tears.

By the time they got to the reception, there wasn't a dry eye in the tent, Sienna's included. She walked across the field to the main house where the restrooms were located so she could touch up her foundation and lipstick.

Another guest came over and stood next to Sienna to wash her hands. "That was the most beautiful wedding ceremony I have ever seen."

"I agree." Sienna nodded, her voice hoarse with emotion.

When she exited the restroom, dinner had begun. Throughout the meal, the deejay kept them entertained with fun clips and activities centered around the bride and groom. Sienna enjoyed the games and festivities, with her favorite being, "How well do you know the bride and groom?"

Finally, the deejay announced it was time for the bouquet toss. Sienna made her way to the edge of the dance floor. She would have stayed where she was if Joel hadn't come over to egg her on, firing up her competitive spirit.

"It's in the bag," she bragged, giving him a thumbs-up.

Sienna scooted closer to the front. She could hear some of the shorter, smaller girls fussing behind her and bit back a grin. As soon as Marisa threw her hands up behind her, Sienna relied on her past experience as a volleyball player and jumped for the bouquet. She gave a loud whoop when it landed in her hands.

She pumped her fists in victory, ignoring the cutting looks of the other women. Then she struck a pose when she saw Joel had his camera pointed at her.

She strutted over and dared him, "Let's see if you can do the same."

Joel winked and handed her the camera. Then he rolled up his sleeves.

Unlike the women who had spaced themselves out, the men were all huddled together a few feet behind the groom. Since Joel had spent most of the night peering through his camera lens, it felt good to relax and enjoy the celebration as one of the guests.

The countdown began, and Joel had his eyes trained on Tucker's arms. Just before the garter toss, though, Joel turned his head to peek at Sienna to see if she was watching. That was his mistake. By the time he refocused, an arm crossed his view and snatched the bride's garter.

The young man—who was handsome, if you liked the rugged type—was more than happy to extend his arm toward Sienna. Instead of a dance, they paraded the perimeter of the venue amid everyone's applause. The other man was a few inches shorter than Sienna, but he didn't seem to mind. In fact, he bragged at the top of his lungs that he was with one of the prettiest girls in the room.

As if Joel didn't know that. Even from here, he could see her dimples on display.

He kept his eyes on Sienna as she marched along to

the beat. When she waved at him, he lifted a hand and smiled. Not for one second did he let on that on the inside, he was wishing he was the one by her side. And he didn't get why he felt that way. He and Sienna were pretend friends on a pretend date to ward off suitors at the wedding. Still, he stuffed his hands into his pockets and stalked over to the table to gather his camera before deciding to use this opportunity to talk to the groom.

Joel sauntered over to Tucker, who was now seated next to his parents. He had tossed his jacket and unbuttoned his shirt. Marisa had left to change out of her wedding dress, as the couple would soon depart for their honeymoon. Tucker had announced his and Marisa's plans to honeymoon in the Maldives, and the crowd had hollered with glee.

After greeting Tucker's parents, Joel addressed him. "Hey, man. Mind if I talk with you for a few minutes?"

"Sure." Tucker slapped his leg and then stood. They made their way over to the now-empty bridal table. Tucker grabbed a slice of wedding cake and stuffed it into his mouth. He closed his eyes, swallowing the treat in two bites. "Mmm… This is so good. I didn't get a chance to eat all day."

Joel chuckled. "That's understandable." He pulled out his cell phone and opened the Voice Recorder app. "So let me start by asking a common question." He sat in the chair next to Tucker and used one of the napkins to wipe his brow. "How did you know Marisa was the One?"

Tucker laughed. "I didn't. In fact, the first time I saw her, I couldn't stand her. She was a thorn in my side."

Joel's brows rose. "Really? I was sure you would say it was love at first sight."

Tucker scoffed. "More like *annoyance and irritation* at first sight. Every time we were in the same place, we bickered. It was like we couldn't stand each other. If she said A, I said Z. You know what I mean?"

"Yes…" Joel nodded. He *could* relate. Tucker had accurately portrayed Joel's interactions with Sienna. Goose bumps prickled his arms. "So how did you two navigate your way from conflict to…romance?" Joel wasn't looking for love, but if Tucker could give him pointers on how to get along better with Sienna, he was open to hearing about it.

Tucker wiped his brow with the back of his hand. "For me, it was like a switch. A light bulb. Our arguments were a cover-up, a smoke screen blinding me to the truth. You know I work for her father and they are very close, so I was bound to run into her often."

The word *proximity* cemented in his brain.

"And there wasn't one time that we got along. It was like whatever I did and said, she was determined to do the opposite. It seemed like she took pleasure in antagonizing me. But the more we had to work together, the more we realized we had something in common."

A flash of he and Sienna doting on Micah hit Joel's mind.

"Then one day, someone sent Marisa a threatening email, and I went berserk. I couldn't eat, sleep or rest until I found the creep. When I realized she would be okay, everything clicked and fell into place." Tucker snapped his fingers. "Like a jigsaw puzzle. It was like God had used every argument to shape us until we became suited. Until I realized that though I could live without her, I didn't want to." His eyes warmed. "And now I don't have to. I get to spend the rest of my life with that woman."

That was where the advice ended. Joel closed the voice app.

"Do you think you will feel this way ten, twenty, thirty years from now?"

The man didn't hesitate. "I think there will never be enough time for us to be together. She is stuck with me for life."

Joel shook hands with the younger man and walked away, meandering through the crowd. He mulled over Tucker's words, while he got some punch for himself and Sienna, who was back at their table, tapping her feet to the beat.

She was watching the ring bearer and flower girl slide across the dance floor, their clothes and hair askew. Since their parents weren't keeping a watchful eye, the children were helping themselves to several slices of cake. The little girl stuffed her mouth while the boy had cake all over his hair and face. When Sienna laughed at their antics, Joel thought there had never been a sweeter sound.

He handed her the drink. "They are going to have stomachaches if this continues."

Sienna nodded and pointed to five plates of cake on the table. "I already confiscated these."

They shared a laugh.

"I can't wait until Micah is their age to see what he gets up to," Joel said, trying to picture Micah as a toddler. "He is really observant, and I catch him following me with his eyes all the time. Like he's learning my steps so he could do the same thing." He lifted his shoulders. "I know that sounds like I'm reaching a bit, but..."

"No. I agree," Sienna rushed to add. "Those bright eyes of his are taking in everything."

"Greg called. Tessa's awake."

Her eyes brightened. "Oh, that's wonderful." Then her gaze saddened. "That means Micah will be going home soon... I'll miss seeing him." She touched her chest. "I know he has to go, but every time I think about it, my heart aches."

Then, in a flash, Sienna was running over to the girl. It took a beat for Joel to realize the girl was choking. He heard several gasps behind him, and a small crowd gathered. Even the music stopped. Heedless of her dress, Sienna snatched the little girl up and began the Heimlich maneuver.

"She's not breathing..."

"She must have swallowed something..."

For some reason—maybe instinct—Joel lifted his camera and started snapping pictures. He tuned out the shocked murmurs behind him and centered his attention on the woman before him.

His camera whirled, capturing every sequence of the scene. Sienna's hat fell to the floor, but she didn't appear to notice or care. She helped until the little girl spat out a wad of cake on the floor. Eyes wide with fear, the girl began to cry.

"My baby! Oh, goodness. I'm so glad you're okay," the mother said, grabbing her daughter and crying herself.

The father hugged them both and rocked his family.

Then he kissed them both on the tops of their heads. Sienna wiped her hands on her soiled dress, watching their embrace with tears in her eyes.

"We can't thank you enough," the father said, giving Sienna a tight hug. "You're a hero."

"I did what anyone would do." Her voice was a whisper. The crowd broke into spontaneous applause, their relief evident. Sienna's eyes were round and large. Joel could see her face grow red, and she seemed to be uneasy with the praise. Just like when she had won Teacher of the Year.

She hobbled toward him, unsure, before lunging into his arms, overcome. Joel placed his camera on the table and, after a brief hesitation, wrapped his arms around her.

"I thought… I thought…" She couldn't get the words out. Her shoulders trembled against his chest. Then she fell apart. Her tears soaked through his shirt.

"You saved her."

She shook her head. "It was all God. I was so nervous that I was praying and praying. I was moving with sheer adrenaline."

Rubbing his hands across her back, Joel soothed her. "It's all right. It's all right. She's safe now."

A few minutes passed before Sienna stiffened and broke out of his embrace. "I'm sorry for slobbering all over your shirt. I can get it dry-cleaned." She began to smooth out her dress, removing pieces of cake.

"Never mind about the shirt." Joel flicked his index finger on her cheek to remove some of the icing from her face.

Guests began gathering their possessions to depart.

Joel and Sienna did the same. The temperature had cooled, and there was a slight breeze. It was also really dark once they left the tent. He noticed her unsteady gait. "What happened to you?"

"I broke my shoe when I dropped to the floor." She stooped to take off both shoes and began to walk across the grass in her bare feet. "I hope I don't step in something unpleasant."

In a flash, Joel scooped her up, his grip surprisingly strong. Her arms went around his neck, and his camera went around hers. "You didn't have to do that," she said, her head moving from left to right as if she wanted to see if they were attracting attention. "I wasn't fishing."

"Don't worry. I know I'm the last person you would want carrying you, but I'm only doing this because I'll avoid cleaning up something unpleasant in the car."

She leaned her head across his chest. "Don't drop me."

"I've got you," he huffed and straightened his knees.

She giggled, placing a hand over her mouth. "You sound out of breath. Why don't you put me down? I think it's fair to say I don't live off salads, and I weigh more than a hundred pounds."

"I said I'm good. Don't worry about it." He gritted his teeth. If she would just be quiet and let him concentrate on putting one foot in front of the other, he knew he would get her the rest of the way. But she couldn't stay still or quiet.

She squirmed. "If you go down, I go down."

"You just refuse to allow me to do something nice for you. I think you just like arguing with me for the sheer pleasure of arguing."

"I'm not arguing." Now her tone sounded frosty. "I'm

trying to spare you and me the humiliation when you can't carry me the distance."

Joel arrived at the pavement and swallowed his sigh of relief. His lower back ached a little, but after those words, there was no way he was going to release her. Not after that unspoken challenge. Sweat rolled down his brow, and he clamped his lips. The car was ten feet away. Easy peasy.

To prove her wrong, Joel sped up, taking measured breaths.

"You just have to make a point, don't you?"

Her words shot adrenaline through him. He kept up the pace the rest of the way and deposited her next to the Jeep. By this time, it was close to eight thirty. If they left now and got Micah, he would be in Pittsburgh by 2:00 a.m. Then he would have ten hours' sleep until his appointment at noon.

Opening the passenger door with a flourish, Joel executed a sharp bow. "After you, milady."

She folded her arms and stood there. A beat later, he heard two surprising words: "Thank you." Her quietly spoken appreciation made his head shoot up.

He raised a brow.

"I've never been carried like that before." She trailed her soft eyes across his chest and arms. "Ever."

He tightened his muscles and puffed out his chest. "Happy to be of service." He made a mental note to sign up for a membership at Jade's gym once it reopened to increase his upper-body strength. Once he closed the door to the vehicle, Joel stretched his neck and back. If he was sore tomorrow, it would all be worth it to have seen that look of admiration on Sienna's face.

Chapter Thirteen

Joel wasn't only physically strong—he was mentally strong. He had to be, because she could hear him singing to Micah nonstop on the other side of the wall of her hotel room. Maybe it was because Micah was away from his familiar environment, but the infant had been restless. Since they had checked in two hours ago, Sienna doubted Micah had stopped fussing.

She doubted Joel had gotten any sleep either. Sienna lay snuggled under the thick white duvet in her suite at the four-star hotel. Joel was singing some tune—off-key—in the room next to hers. Though she had offered to keep the baby, Joel had been adamant about having Micah stay with him.

His rationalization was that Micah was used to him at night, and he wanted to keep his routine as much as possible. The genius had declared he would simply put the lights out, and all would be well. Sienna had tried her best to keep from yelling that Micah was a baby, not a bird. He had no clue about day or night. Now none of them were getting any rest after the five-hour trek.

At least he had allowed her to drive for two of those hours so he could sleep.

She heard a little wail and threw off the covers. Shoving her feet into her slippers, she grabbed her room key card and stomped to the next room. Mindful of other sleeping guests, she rapped on the door. Seconds later, it swung open, and her mouth dropped.

Joel was still dressed in the same clothes, except his previously pristine shirt was hanging outside of his slacks, stained with milk and tears. His hair could give Albert Einstein some competition, and his eyes had dark circles a raccoon would envy.

Once she had entered her room, Sienna had taken the time to shower and dress in a pair of cotton short pajamas with the word *BeYoutiful* across the chest.

If he had just listened to her, he would be sleeping. The stubborn man was exhausted, and if he didn't get some rest now, he wouldn't be able to stay awake for his interview in the next few hours. Concern for Joel, and the fact that Micah was still dressed in his shorts and T-shirt from yesterday, made her fury rise.

She held out her hands without saying a word. He placed Micah gently in her arms. He was wrapped in his blanket, and his little face was covered in sweat. Even his clothes felt damp. The room felt like a sauna, which meant Joel must have turned off the air conditioner.

Yes, the rooms had been really cold when they arrived, but no wonder the baby was crying.

After rolling her eyes, she pointed to the diaper bag. Sienna refused to start speaking, because she knew she wouldn't be able to keep her voice lowered. He went to do her bidding.

"Do you want me to—"

She shook her head, lifted a finger and placed it over her mouth. He clamped his jaw and placed the bag on her shoulders. Then, with a nod, Sienna silently went back to her room. Micah snuggled into her chest, and her ire cooled.

Holding him in the crook of her arm, she bolted the safety locks and then padded across the carpet to the king-size bed. She spread out his blanket and rested the infant in the middle of the bed. "It's all right, little man. I'll get you all comfy in no time."

First, she adjusted the room temperature; then she washed her hands. While she worked, she hummed. Next, she undressed Micah, then retrieved a couple of baby wipes and wiped him down. It might have been her imagination, but Micah gave her a little smile. Once she'd rubbed him down with some lavender lotion, she put him in a new diaper and slipped a clean onesie over him. Once she closed the clasp, Micah emitted a yawn.

"There now. You should be able to get some rest. Your uncle must not realize that you're human and able to feel overheated, even if you can't express it." She cuddled the baby close to her chest and rocked him to sleep. He let out a contented sigh, which tugged at her heart, and she touched his cheek.

Then she laid the baby next to her on the bed, and her eyes fluttered closed.

Joel hurried up the driveway to stand next to Sienna as she rang the doorbell to her parents' home. The hotel was about fifteen minutes away from their house, and the closer they'd gotten to their destination, the quieter she had become. He could see her chewing on her bottom lip and figured she was fretting about the reception she'd receive from them.

He refrained from trying to engage her in conversation, feeling the tension flow off her body. He assumed she needed to prepare mentally before seeing the Kings. While they waited for the door to open, Joel asked her if she was okay, and she gave him a terse nod.

They had booked the hotel rooms for two nights, so their bags and personal items were still at the hotel. He had Micah in his carrier in one hand and the diaper bag in the other.

A tall gentleman, who he assumed was Sienna's dad, answered the door. Joel had been a second grader when he had met Sienna's parents, but he didn't remember them. The Kings weren't the type of parents who had shown up to school or town events often.

"Hi, Dad," Sienna said, her voice shaky.

Mr. King's mouth dropped. "Sienna. You're here." He gave his daughter a hug—rocking her back and forth, patting her on the back before breaking the embrace. Then he glanced Joel's way, and his gaze dropped to the carrier. His eyes narrowed and he frowned, but he held his tongue.

Pointing his way, Sienna made introductions. After a brief hesitation, Mr. King—Lennox, as he had instructed Joel to call him—moved aside to let them inside. He followed Sienna into the living room area. His eyes were immediately drawn to a few pieces done in mosaic art on the wall. Joel took a seat on the couch next to Sienna, who gestured for him to set Micah next to her. He reached into the bag and took out a baby blanket.

Lennox slipped into the armchair across from them, observing their movements. Joel realized he and Sienna were moving in a way that indicated they had done this several times. And Lennox noticed.

"Where's Mom?" Sienna asked, placing the blanket on her lap and then taking Micah out of the carrier. She held the sleeping baby across her chest. His head lolled back, and his mouth was open.

Joel wished he could sleep through this awkward moment too. He and Sienna had agreed to go to her parents' home so that he would have about an hour to get acquainted with them as her "boyfriend" before leaving for the interview at the rookie camp. They had stopped in the hotel lobby to have some breakfast before heading to her parents' neighborhood.

"She went on an errand." Lennox glanced at his watch. "She should be back any minute. If you had told me you were coming, I would've grilled steaks or something."

"I didn't want you doing too much." Sienna turned toward Joel. "No one makes steaks like my daddy."

Pointing to the mosaic art, Joel said, "The artwork and detail on the tiles are incredible."

Lennox quirked his lips. "Thank you. It's a hobby I started a few years ago. After a tough case in court, I find it relaxing."

Joel felt his eyes go wide. "You made those?"

"Yes."

"You are a man of many talents." Joel listened, fascinated, as Lennox started talking about the process, and his design and method for applying the tiles. Joel caught Sienna's eye.

With a twinkle in her eyes, she touched her nose. She was calling him a brownnoser. Joel ignored the barb and returned his attention to her father, who was still talking. The front door opened, and Sienna stiffened. Lennox got to his feet to greet his wife. Joel gripped the chair, preparing himself for the mother-daughter reunion.

She hadn't yet registered their presence. "Somebody parked their Jeep in front of our driveway. So I had to park on the next block." Joel took in the tall, regal woman wearing a scarf on her head and a pair of slacks with a cardigan. Sienna was her carbon copy. They had the same complexion, voice and deep dimples. Then she took the scarf off, revealing a smooth buzz cut, and gasped.

Her head turned toward them in slow motion at the same time Lennox said, "Honey, it's—"

"Sienna!" Daphne stepped back and touched her chest. "You gave me a scare." The scarf fell to the floor. Her voice broke, and she patted her head, appearing self-conscious. Then her lips curled. "I told you not to come." She gave Joel a shy smile before her eyes fell on a sleeping Micah.

Joel looked at Sienna expectantly, waiting for her to introduce him, but her eyes were glued to her mom, her mouth ajar. "Your—your hair. You didn't tell me..." Her words were choppy, like she was gasping for air. Meanwhile, her mother had dropped into a nearby chair, covering her head with her hands.

Lennox was by his wife's side, uttering soothing words, offering comfort.

Acting on instinct, Joel reached over to touch

Sienna's shoulder. Goose bumps popped up where he made contact. "Are you okay?"

She tensed before she shook her head, mumbling incoherently under her breath and dabbing at her eyes. He reached over to scoop Micah off her lap. Micah started to fuss. Joel rested the baby on his shoulder and patted his back. When he glanced over at Daphne, he noticed her gaze was now centered on him.

With a start, he realized that with all the commotion, he hadn't been introduced. "Hello, Mrs. King. I'm Joel. Sienna's…uh…boyfriend." His words fell flat for a beat, but then he saw Daphne's eyes go wide.

She pointed her index finger at him. "'Boyfriend'? But—you have a newborn." She bunched her fists and jumped to her feet. Then she tugged Sienna up to stand. "It's good to meet you, Joel. But please excuse me while I have a word with my daughter. Alone."

Sienna trudged behind the formidable woman, sparing Joel a pleading glance and mouthing the words "I'm sorry." Her posture was one of preparing for a showdown, with the certainty that they were entering a battle they couldn't win. Seeing the sassy woman he knew appearing so tame roused his worry.

Lennox cleared his throat. "They'll work it out." The fact that he sounded unbothered put Joel at ease. Somewhat. "How about I show you my mosaic workshop? Everything is set up in the shed outside."

"I'd love to see it." Joel reached into the diaper bag and pulled out the baby carrier to secure Micah to his chest. Then he followed Lennox into the backyard. Since they passed in the same direction as Sienna and her mother, he strained his ears for raised voices but heard nothing. Joel heaved a sigh of relief. Maybe his concern had been ill-founded. Mother and daughter were probably hugging it out, and he had been worried for nothing. Feeling optimistic, Joel concentrated on fulfilling his role as the dutiful boyfriend by getting to know Sienna's father a little better.

Chapter Fourteen

As soon as they were in her parents' bedroom, chosen because of the soundproof walls, her mother ripped into her. "What on earth are you thinking to date a man with a newborn? And where's the baby's mother?" Without waiting for a response, Daphne started pacing.

Sienna knew from experience that she would have to let Daphne release her shock before she would be able to explain. So she settled in the chaise longue to wait her mother out. She sat cross-legged and folded her arms, trying to contain her own surprise at her mother's shaved head. Daphne took pride in her tresses, so for her to have cut off her hair…it meant… No, she didn't want to think about what that meant.

Daphne continued, "The baby can't be more than a month, at most. I mean, what were you thinking?" She gasped, placed a hand on her hip before spinning to face Sienna. "Is he a widower? He must be." Rushing over to join her daughter on the chair, she took her hand. "That makes sense. I'm sorry for jumping to conclusions. That must be tough for him." Her voice now held compassion.

Sienna rubbed between her eyes. Her mother's gamut of emotions could be exhausting. "Mom. Micah—that's the baby's name—is Joel's nephew. He's been taking care of him for his brother for a few weeks, and I'm helping him."

Her mother heaved a sigh filled with relief. But then her brow creased. "'Helping'? I don't understand. How do you have time to help with an infant when you have your dissertation to do?"

"I love babies, and I wanted to help," she said, through gritted teeth while praying for a double dose of patience. Five minutes in her parents' presence, and her mother was making her feel like she was six years old all over again. And finding fault.

Daphne nodded. "I love your generous spirit, Sienna, but you have to concentrate on yourself. That's the joy of being single—you get to make choices."

"Yes. And I made the choice to help Joel take care of a helpless infant. One whose mother is in a coma and whose father is worried out of his mind."

Holding up a hand, Daphne relented. "I get it. I get it. I'm sorry for jumping to conclusions." She shifted her position and then gave her a cheeky smile. "Joel's really cute."

Sienna couldn't hide her disbelief. "What? When did you have time to register how he looks?"

Daphne patted her hand. "Oh, I'm good at multitasking like that. And he's a keeper."

Her mother was a trip. Sienna chuckled. "So now that he's single—without a child—he's cute and a keeper." She shook her head. "I don't understand your logic."

"Any man who would jump to help take care of a

newborn must be selfless and caring. Both good traits in a husband."

"Whoa. Slow down. I'm not looking for a husband," Sienna sputtered. "And if I were, it certainly wouldn't be…" She stopped, realizing she had been about to say Joel's name.

"Wouldn't be what?" her mother asked.

"Uh… It certainly wouldn't be until I am Dr. King."

"No reason why it couldn't be both Dr. and Mrs. Whatever."

Unfolding her legs and scooting to the edge of the chair, Sienna ignored that comment and asked the burning question: "Mom, what happened to your hair?" Her heart hammered in her chest while she waited for her mother to respond.

As if she had forgotten that she had shaved her hair, Daphne patted her head. Sienna could see the tears fill her mother's eyes, and her heart twisted.

After licking her lips, Daphne croaked out, "I shaved it."

Sienna raised a brow. "When? You didn't tell me you were doing chemo. I just spoke to you a couple days ago, and you had a head full of hair." She shook her head and asked gently, "Is that why you wanted me to stay away?"

Her mother swallowed several times, like she was struggling to maintain her composure. "I'm not doing chemo. I did this in an act of defiance." Daphne straightened. "I was… I was angry and hurt. I… I know I don't have much time left and…" She bunched her fists. "I didn't know what to do, so I grabbed your father's razor and…" She lifted her shoulders and then exhaled. "It was scary, but after the first shock, it felt good. It felt really good." Her voice didn't hold an ounce of regret.

"But your hair was your glory. You've repeated that to me so many times that I hear it in my head whenever I have the temptation to get a pixie cut. In fact, I know you hate that I often hide mine in braids."

Daphne's face grew grave. "Yeah, well. I'm learning that when death starts knocking, you have no problem letting things go. The things you thought were gigantic become small, insignificant. Minuscule. Because one day, you'll have to leave everything behind, whether you want to or not. Whether you're ready or not." She jutted her chin. "Shaving my head gave me some measure of control. Choice."

Her words sank in. Sienna waved a hand. "You could've just colored your hair."

Daphne chuckled. "I guess you have a point. But now that I am free of the hassle of maintaining the perfect hairdo, I don't know why I held on to it that long." Then she gave Sienna a look of uncertainty. "Do you like it?"

Sienna nodded. In a way, she felt like her mother was talking about more than the perfect head of hair. Daphne's words made Sienna think of the past, of regret. Of pain and hurt. And she realized she, too, didn't want to keep walking in that. It was a burden. And it was time she freed herself.

She looked at her mother through the clear lens of the present, no longer focused on the past. "I love it because I love you. You're beautiful, no matter what."

Tears ran down Daphne's face. "I scared an old man at the grocery store just now. Went to get some ice cream, and when he saw me, he started blinking and pointing. I was so embarrassed that I rushed out of the store, put the scarf on my head and returned home. When I walked in, I felt like I had made the biggest mistake of my life."

"It's just hair. It doesn't define you." Sienna squeezed Daphne's shoulder. She didn't think she had ever seen her mother so unsure and vulnerable. "It doesn't take away from the fact that you're an accomplished harpist in big demand."

Daphne took her hand. Sienna felt a slight tremble and used her other hand to cup her mother's.

"Will you go with me back to the store?" her mother asked in a small voice. "I could eat some rocky road."

The thought of her mother needing her made Sienna straighten. "Yes. I'd be happy to go. We'll go together."

Daphne touched Sienna's cheek. "I'm so glad you came. I'm so glad you didn't listen to me. I needed to see you."

Sienna's heart expanded. "I'm glad too."

Pulling on her dangling earring in her left ear, Daphne was back in charge. "And while we're on our way, you can fill me in on your relationship with Joel. You two seemed chummy when I walked through the door."

Relationship. With Joel. Those three words made her feet feel leaden. Burdened by their deception. "I don't have much to say." Guilt churned within her. Sienna didn't feel right about her and Joel's plan after this open conversation with her mother. The only way she could deal with her guilt was to lead the conversation in a new direction. "How about I talk about how to improve my dissertation so I pass my defense?"

That was a topic her mother couldn't resist. With an

eager nod, Daphne said, "I'll be your sounding board," and started toward the door.

Sienna trailed after her mother, glad that she had shifted the topic away from Joel for now. But the words *relationship with Joel* stayed with her, scared her because of the curiosity they had awakened. The curiosity of whether or not they could be more than sparring partners and occasional friends. The curiosity of why, whenever they'd made physical contact, an interest stirred. She knew she had to tamp down on that before she started yearning for something that could never be.

The interview was a bust. The kid was a no-show. Turned out that Jayvaughn had decided to accept another offer from another football team instead; Joel had shown up to the Pittsburgh Steelers rookie camp for nothing. He hurried back to his Jeep to call Skip and let him know what had transpired. Or rather, *not* transpired.

Skip was not pleased. "That generation can be so fickle and lacks responsibility. All he had to do was call and give us a heads-up instead of dropping the news on social media. I hate that. Now I need a filler for Wednesday's edition. What else do you have?"

Joel's heart rate increased. Skip was expecting him to have a solution on the spot. Joel needed another article idea, fast. Every action that he took until Skip retired was considered an informal interview for the editor in chief position. Joel flipped through the notes in his phone. "I still have the piece on the mayor's wedding that you decided not to run yesterday."

"Naw. I'm saving that for the end of the month, when

we do the wedding special. I need something edgier to sell papers on hump day." He could hear Skip snap his fingers. "That kid was supposed to be our feel-good hero story, and now we have a gaping hole. It will be your duty to fill that gap."

Joel massaged his temples, feeling the pressure to think on the spot. "I could do..." His eyes went wide, and his brain caught on the word *hero*. Hero. Sienna saving that child was a hero story. One that warmed his heart every time he thought about it. His stomach knotted. Sienna would never agree to the story—but they had come a long way in their friendship these past few weeks. Maybe if he asked her and explained his situation, she would relent.

"Well?" Skip demanded.

"Give me an hour. I have an idea."

"The clock is ticking." With that, Skip ended the call. The plan had been for Joel to return to the Kings' house to join Sienna and her parents for dinner after he was finished with the interview. Once Sienna and her mother had returned from their private tête-à-tête, the air in the room had lightened.

Sitting in his Jeep, Joel's fingers flew across the keyboard of his laptop. The words flowed through him. Forty-five minutes later, he attached the article, along with a few pictures from the wedding, and pressed Send after adding in the body of the email that Skip should wait until Joel had received permission before going to press. Joel raced out of the parking lot, back to the Kings' home. He intended for Sienna to read and approve the article and then have Skip post it.

Joel found himself looking forward to getting to

know Sienna's family—and of course, seeing Micah. He sent Sienna a text to let her know he was on his way back. Sienna had already texted him pictures of Micah, with those piercing bright eyes of his trained on the camera, making Joel wonder what he was thinking. Wait. Did babies think? And if so, what did they think about?

He continued his random musings to deflect from his nervousness over Sienna's response to his favor. Before he knew it, he was pulling in in front of her parents' home, and he hadn't found the words to ask her.

Joel bounded up the three steps and pressed the doorbell. Seconds later, the door swung open, and Sienna's smiling face appeared. His heart skipped a beat, and he lost his breath. Sienna King was beautiful. Tongue-tied, he returned her grin while he struggled to remember how to greet her like he normally would so she wouldn't suspect what he was really thinking right then.

"I'm sorry to hear your interview fell through," she said, eyes beaming, as she stepped aside to allow him to enter, clueless that his mouth and brain refused to cooperate.

She sees you as a friend, he reminded himself. And even that was pushing it.

Then he heard Micah's cry. That spurred him into action, and he hurried inside to see his nephew. Joel stopped short. Daphne was holding him in her arms, and Lennox was right next to her, playing with Micah's feet.

"It's a good thing you came back when you did, because we're tempted to kidnap him," Daphne cooed, her eyes on the infant.

"Yeah, I battle those thoughts every day," Joel said. Grateful for the smooth comeback, he decided he would avoid making eye contact with Sienna until he recalibrated in his mind that there couldn't be more between them. He was one step above a nuisance in her eyes. And anyway, he didn't want more. He didn't need any more potential heartbreak.

Sienna sidled next to him, and the smell of apricots teased his senses. She spoke to him in a conspiratorial tone. "They've been like this since you left. I haven't been able to hold him even once."

His heart beat fast in his chest at her proximity. What on earth was happening right now?

"Oh, yeah..." he sputtered. Words failed him as he grappled with this new and unwelcome sensation. He didn't want to feel this drawn to anyone, especially not Sienna.

Inching away from her, Joel went to sit in the love seat across from her parents. But she came to sit right next to him. He gave her the side-eye. He wouldn't put it past her to sense his sudden attraction and make him suffer with the gentle grazing of her arm next to his.

"I'd better go check on those steaks," Lennox said and stood. "Be right back."

Joel offered to assist, his tone slightly panicked: "I can help you."

But Lennox waved him off. "Naw. It's your first time here. You're a guest." Then he pointed and joked, "The next time you come, I'll put you to work." He sauntered out of the room.

He tensed, half expecting Sienna to chime in with "There won't be a next time," but all she did was giggle.

Joel turned to look at her, forgetting his decision to avoid meeting that gaze, those long lashes and... *Stop.*

This wasn't an attraction. It was gratitude. He mustn't confuse the two. "What are you laughing at?" His question came off sharper than he'd anticipated, but all of a sudden, she had him on edge.

"What?" She shrugged. "That was funny."

"You're being a daddy's girl."

Her eyes went wide. "I am, aren't I? That's new for me."

Seeing that she was in such a good mood, Joel decided to use that opportunity to talk with her about the article. He spoke quickly and fast, glad Daphne was there as a buffer to keep Sienna from exploding.

Breathless, he rattled on that Skip was waiting on her agreement and that there would be a nominal fee for her doing the article. When he was finished, he held his breath while Sienna chewed her bottom lip and considered it.

She shrank into the couch. "I don't like the spotlight..."

At least she hadn't turned him down flat. He told himself to stay silent, give her time to think.

Her mother, however, had no qualms about sharing her opinion. "I think that's wonderful," Daphne said, beaming. "In my world, there's no such thing as bad press."

"I'm not in your world, Mom." Sienna angled her head toward him and then squared her shoulders. "I'll do it."

He felt his eyes go wide. "You'll do it?"

She nodded, lowering her head and smoothing her pants.

Her choice of words put him at ease. That was his feisty Sienna. "Thank you so much." Joel pulled her in for a hug. Her arms somehow got folded between them, but she didn't tense up. She curved into him and lifted her head. He drew in a breath at what he saw reflected in her brown orbs.

So he pulled back, swallowing his disappointment and calling himself a punk.

Judging by the heavy sigh from Sienna's mother, Joel would say she agreed that he was a punk. But at least he was a punk out of danger of falling into the love zone. But if he was out of danger, why didn't he feel the least bit relieved?

Micah's cry cut into the quiet. The infant squirmed and placed his little fist in his mouth, sucking hard.

"Uh-oh. Somebody's hungry," Daphne said with a little laugh. Micah, however, wasn't amused. He scrunched his face and let out a bigger wail, his little chest heaving.

Joel started to stand, but Sienna grabbed his arm. "I've got it."

He didn't miss Sienna's reddened face when she excused herself. He watched her scurry out of the room and thought that he would feel relieved. Relieved that he hadn't given in to his instincts. But all he felt was… empty.

Chapter Fifteen

Sienna's motto was, *If you can't be honest with yourself, then how can you be honest with others?* That was why—as she stood in Joel's home a couple of days later, prepping Micah's bottle—she admitted she was still furious with herself for wanting Joel to kiss her. Not that she would ever let him know that.

Truth be told, she didn't even know where that had sprung from. But she had pushed it back to the far recesses of her mind and had done her best to act unbothered since. Fortunately, Joel had played along. Neither one had brought it up. Besides, she had other pressing matters, like her dissertation, to focus on. Sienna had been given a tentative date of July 8 to defend it again, and her professor had sent her some tough questions to answer.

She measured enough powder into the bottle to make about four ounces before pouring in the special filtered water, closing it and giving it a good shake. Sienna and Joel had switched Micah's formula to one that didn't cause as much gas after that gut-wrenching crying incident. He hadn't had a problem since. She plugged in the bottle warmer and put the bottle inside.

It was close to noon and almost time for Micah's nap. While the bottle warmed, she would give him a bath so that once he had his bottle, he would be ready for bed. That had been Jade and Kelsey's advice: Bath, bottle, bed. In that order. It worked every time.

Humming a praise song, Sienna put the oven to preheat to 425 degrees. She planned to put on some frozen chicken teriyaki thighs and make a quick salad. Joel intended to be home for lunch and would watch Micah for a few hours while she worked on her dissertation. He had an event at the town library he wanted to cover that evening, and Sienna would stay with Micah until he returned.

They had a good system worked out.

At exactly twelve thirty, Sienna had Micah bathed, dressed in a onesie and drinking his bottle. The chicken teriyaki was hot and ready, and the salad was cooling in the fridge.

Joel opened the door and sniffed the air. "Smells like you're cooking some good food in here."

"It's not homemade, so don't get too excited." She chuckled.

He rubbed his stomach. "Still, you warmed it. So that counts for something." He washed his hands and then came over to where she sat on the couch. "Do you need me to take the little guy?"

Feeling territorial, Sienna hugged Micah close. He had one hand wrapped around her thumb, and he was looking at her with such trust in his eyes, she didn't want to part ways with him just yet. "I've got him.

Why don't you get the salad and dressing out of the refrigerator?"

"On it." He did as she'd asked and set everything on the table.

Micah took his last chug, and Sienna patted his back. Seconds later, he emitted a loud burp. His eyes were heavy with sleep.

"Show them how it's done, Micah!" Joel yelled, holding a fist in the air.

Micah jolted awake. His little body shook, and his lower lip quivered.

"Oh no. Look what you've done," Sienna said, hoping Micah would settle. But a loud wail followed.

Joel whispered. "I'm sorry."

She rolled her eyes. "No point in whispering now. He's up." Micah's arms jerked with fury at his interrupted nap. "He's too worked up to go to sleep."

Joel took the crying infant out of her arms. "I'm sorry, Micah. I didn't mean to startle you." His words only seemed to make the baby scream even louder.

Sienna went into the front room and grabbed the stroller. Then she indicated to Joel to place Micah inside. "The fresh air might soothe him. Enjoy your lunch." Then she was through the door. As soon as Micah felt the sun on his face, he squinted and scrunched his nose, but the tears ceased. Sienna lowered the stroller cover so he would have some shade.

"You don't think he will get too hot?" Joel asked.

Spinning around, she touched her chest. "You don't have to come. I'm only going around the block. You need to eat because you skipped breakfast this morning."

"If you're not eating, then *we're* not eating." He

pushed his cap farther up his head and tried to grab the stroller handle, but Sienna held up a hand.

"Must we argue?" she said, shifting so they both could fit behind the handle. Pulling on her sunglasses, which had been hooked on the collar of her shirt, Sienna started walking. It was a tight and awkward fit, but they navigated the sidewalk together. After they bumped into each other, and Sienna had gotten jostled one too many times, she relented and let Joel take the lead. They crossed to the opposite side of the street so they could see oncoming traffic since there were no sidewalks in this part of town. While they walked, Sienna talked about her day with Micah.

It was a lovely day out, and their brisk walk did a lot to calm Micah. She could hear him gurgling and cooing.

"This was a good idea," Joel said. "I could have used this tip early in the morning."

"You don't use the swing?" Her voice held surprise.

"No, I keep forgetting to use that. I hold him against my chest."

"You didn't forget. You just like holding him. Admit it." Sienna gave him the side-eye.

Joel laughed. "Maybe. Just a little bit. I love feeling him curl against me."

"Hmm… Let's see if you still feel that way when you need to put him down and can't because he is crying his eyes out."

"I'm not worried about it." He shrugged. "I'll just hand him to you."

She gave him a light shove. "Nope. You're going to keep him since you insist on spoiling him."

"Quit acting like you don't do the same thing. I see

you holding him even when he's been asleep for a good while."

By then, they were halfway down the block. She placed a hand over her eyes. Up ahead, a brown Toyota Camry inched its way toward them. She huddled closer to Joel and placed a hand on the stroller.

The windows rolled down, and the person inside the vehicle raised a hand in greeting. Sienna squinted. He looked familiar, but the glare from the sun shielded his features from her view. Beside her, Joel stiffened, rooted into place. Sienna tilted her head to look over at him. "What's wrong? You know him?"

All Joel could do was point at the stranger. Seeing words elude the man who gabbed for a living made her heart race. The only occupant in the vehicle leaned over. She clearly saw the person behind the wheel. Sienna gasped; the resemblance to Joel was striking. This had to be Joel's brother. She placed a hand over her mouth before gripping Joel's arm. If his brother was here, then that would mean…it was time for Micah to go home.

Sienna looked down at Micah's adorable face. There was no way she was ready to let him go.

His time with Micah was over. For now. So many conflicting emotions raced through Joel. Happiness for Micah mingled with relief at Tessa's recovery. But beneath it all was a minor ache at what his brother's presence meant. Joel's chest constricted, but he forced his face to relax into a smile. Giving Sienna's arm a reassuring pat, he shuffled over to the car.

"Hey, bro," Greg greeted, putting the car in Park and hopping out of the vehicle. He left the door ajar and rushed around to where Joel stood. "Tessa and I couldn't go another day without our son, so I jumped on a flight early this morning. I hope you don't mind me barging in on you like this, but I imagine you must be eager to get back to your life."

His lonely, meaningless life…

"N-N-No." Joel cleared his throat. "I told you, you're welcome anytime. I wish you'd told me you were coming. I could've met you at the airport." And he would have had time to mentally prepare himself…and Sienna.

"I tried calling but I had a poor signal, so I texted you. Maybe my texts didn't go through. I drove to Dallas and caught a red-eye to Baltimore. I was on standby, so I wasn't sure I would get on. Then there was a mix-up with the rental and an accident on the highway, or I would've been here earlier." He gave Joel a quick hug and glanced at his watch. "I'm due back at the airport in a couple hours. I can't wait to be with my son." He darted over to Micah.

A couple hours... They wouldn't have time to say goodbye. His brother sure was in a rush. Joel understood why, but his heart protested. It was too soon.

Sienna stepped aside to make space for Greg. Joel made quick introductions, ignoring the tears sheening her eyes. He didn't know if she was emotional about the reunion or if, like him, she was ruing that their time with Micah had come to an end.

After returning the greeting, Greg bent over to play with Micah's feet. "Daddy's here. Daddy's here. Look at how big you've gotten. I missed you so much." All his attention was on his child. Despite the sun's relentless rays beating on his face and arms, Greg remained focused on Micah, who was observing his father with keen eyes. Then Micah did something that made Joel's heart turn to putty.

Micah smiled. A smile that made Joel's heart expand with awe…and jealousy. A smile that was precious and priceless. It was like Micah had been saving that for his father's return. Sienna reached for her cell phone and captured the moment, freezing it in time.

Overcome, Joel wiped his eyes. "Wow. That's a first."

"Did you see that? He just smiled." Greg rubbed Micah's tummy. "Are you smiling for Daddy, son?"

Joel heard a sniffle and saw Sienna wipe her face with her hands. Then she whispered in his ear, "Let me go get him packed. I'll see you back inside." With a pat, she left the brothers alone with her arms wrapped around herself. Her gait was slow, and Joel deduced that the thought of saying goodbye was too much. At least Sienna could retreat to grieve Micah's imminent departure. Joel would have to do that…later. For now, his heart rejoiced at the sheer joy on his brother's face.

He took charge. "Let's get you inside, out of the heat." He went to turn the stroller around, but Greg got there first. Joel's eyes met Greg's. Of course his brother would take the reins, so to speak; Micah was his son. With a brief dip of the head, Joel gestured for Greg to proceed, stating his house number. "I'll pull the rental into the driveway."

The sudden shift from chief provider back to uncle jarred his psyche. From inside the rental car, Joel watched his brother strut down the sidewalk, his steps bouncy and light, as he talked with Micah.

Joel gripped the wheel. "Keep it together. You knew once Tessa awakened that it would be time for Micah to go home." But he didn't know his heart would feel like it had been ripped apart, and Micah hadn't even left yet. Drawing a deep breath, he eased his foot off the brake, put the car in gear and drove the short distance to the driveway.

Before going in, Joel took a few minutes to gather himself. What if he hadn't returned home for lunch today? Joel would have gotten a phone call from Sienna telling him that Micah was gone. He wouldn't have had the chance to hold Micah in his arms and kiss that soft, tiny cheek. But he did have that chance, and he was wasting precious time in this car when he could be hugging his nephew and taking some pictures.

With sudden urgency, Joel raced inside the house.

Chapter Sixteen

Her hands were shaky, her breath choppy and her insides felt hollow. Empty. Sienna felt the pain of Micah's leaving deep inside. Standing in his nursery, she stuffed his diaper bag with all his essentials, willing herself not to cry.

Joel had dashed inside and clambered up the stairs to get his camera. Then he began snapping pictures. There had to have been at least a hundred of her and Micah, Joel and Micah. Micah alone. She had lost count before she excused herself to gather Micah's belongings. She slung the strap on her shoulders and returned to the living area.

"Thank you so much for everything you did for Micah," Greg said to her. Once he had stepped inside the house, Greg had scooped his son up in his arms and settled on the couch to cuddle with him, showering his cheeks with love and kisses.

She placed the diaper bag on the couch while Greg rambled on, oblivious that she was seconds away from falling apart. She went into the kitchen to make Micah a couple of bottles for his journey home.

"Thanks again," he said.

Sienna cupped her stomach. "You're welcome, but it wasn't a problem at all."

"Still, you must be grateful to get back to your life. I know when I was single, I didn't want to be shackled to a child."

She stole a glance over at Joel, who had lowered his camera, somberly watching his brother and Micah interact.

Sienna lifted her chin. "I felt none of those things. I'm an educator, so children are a part of my life and livelihood. I loved every minute of it." Her voice cracked. "Your son is a treasure."

Her arms ached to hold Micah. Sienna stepped forward, hesitant. She didn't want Greg seeing how difficult it was to see Micah go. She didn't want to be selfish, ruining the overjoyed father's reunion with his son. But she hadn't had any warning.

"I so agree." Greg brought Micah close to his chest and kissed his forehead. Micah started to cry, and Sienna had to fight the urge to pull him out of his father's arms. As if reading her mind, Greg stood and held the crying infant out to her.

Without hesitation, Sienna accepted Micah and rocked him. "It's all right, little guy." She cooed and hummed her favorite praise tune to him. Her heart constricted when Micah stopped crying and snuggled into her chest.

"Micah loves when she sings that," Joel told Greg.

"Noted. He'll get used to me and Tessa again," Greg said, seemingly more to himself than to his brother. He took the diaper bag and slung it over his shoulder.

"Whoa. This weighs a ton." Picking up the car seat, he went toward the front door.

"Micah accumulated a lot during his stay here," Joel said, following behind Greg to take the car seat out of his hand. "Let me help you with this. It can be tricky getting it situated in the car."

"I appreciate that. I'm sorry I can't take the rest of his stuff with me. We have his room set up already, or I'd have you ship everything to me. Maybe you can save it for your own child."

Save it for your own child... Sienna's eyes met Joel's. His brows furrowed, and his eyes were wide, as if the off-handed suggestion had punched him in the gut. If she weren't so heartbroken at Micah's departure, Sienna would have laughed or used that moment to tease Joel about his panicked expression.

Greg pushed the screen door, holding it open for Joel to pass him.

Joel croaked out an unsure-sounding "I guess," and walked outside.

She ambled over to the door with Micah tucked under her arm, watching the brothers pack the rental with only the bare necessities. Tomorrow, she would call the women's shelter to see if they would do a pickup. Scanning the room with all the baby paraphernalia still left behind made her heart twist.

Waves and waves of realization hit her. She sucked in a breath. This was the last time she would cradle Micah close, hear his sounds, inhale his special smell. Tears overflowed, trekking down her cheeks. A sob broke free. Seeing Joel and Greg coming back inside, she turned her back to the door to head to the nursery.

"Sienna."

She froze.

Joel's tortured voice was her undoing. She returned Micah to his father. "Safe travels," she said before rushing into the bathroom. She couldn't stand there and watch Greg drive off with the tiny bundle who held a huge place in her heart. Locking the door, she released her agony. Her shoulders shook under the weight of her tears—tears she felt came from her bowels to her soul—until she collapsed to the floor. She wished she had had the guts to give Micah one more kiss before he departed. Regret for her cowardice made her sorrow increase.

"I'm never going to see him again. I'm never going to see him again," Sienna sobbed until she heard a rap on the door.

She washed her face, her hands trembling, and opened the door to see Joel's grief-stricken face. Sudden anger roared like a lion within her, and she pummeled Joel's chest with her fists like he was a punching bag. "I told you I didn't want to do this," she raged. "I didn't want to get too close. You should have gotten a professional to watch Micah. Someone who…who wouldn't care." She hiccupped.

Joel held her hands in his. "I knew this day would come. I knew Micah would have to go home. But I didn't know it would feel like this." He lowered his head and leaned against the doorjamb, as if he needed it to hold up his weight. "I didn't know it would feel like someone ripped my heart out."

She paused a beat as the visual imagery evoked by his words soaked in.

He raised a brow. “Too much?”

“Yes. You need to edit. Because that was just extra.”

They shared a laugh, releasing some of the tension caused by Micah’s departure.

Then to her surprise, Joel leaned over to rest his head on her shoulder. Her arms went around him to keep them balanced. The scent of sweat, pine and sandalwood teased her nostrils. She patted his back, lifting her chin and tilting her head to accommodate his dead weight.

“I’m trying to be sensitive, but I don’t know how long I can maintain this,” she huffed out when it appeared as if Joel had no intention of easing up.

He jumped up, and she felt the loss of his closeness right away. “I’m sorry. It’s comforting being with someone who gets how I’m feeling right now.”

“I know.” She wiped her face. “And what a sorry pair we make.”

“I don’t get how such a marvelous day could end so…”

“Horrible?” she supplied.

His lips quirked. “I don’t think we can say it’s horrible, because Micah is going back home, where he belongs. That’s great for him, but it’s awful for us.” He scoffed. “The entire time I was out there putting in the car seat, Greg kept thanking me over and over. He offered to reimburse me for all the things I purchased. I declined, of course, but while he went on and on, I was fighting with myself not to grab Micah and run.”

“Yeah, I can see the headlines now.” Sienna splayed her hands. “‘Nephew Kidnapped by Local Town Reporter and Nuisance.’ It would hit national news.”

"I can see you laughing at the irony." Despite his words, Joel gave her a tender look.

"I'd probably join you..." She trailed off, mesmerized by the look in Joel's eyes.

The small space in the bathroom suddenly felt confining. She rubbed her eyes, feeling a headache coming on. Sienna stepped out and into the hallway before facing him. "Here's something that should make you feel better—with Micah gone, I won't be babysitting for you anymore, and so this releases you from being my wedding date." Sienna kept her tone playful. "You can be happy about that, at least."

Like a needle and thread, disappointment sewed its way into her heart. Sienna clamped her jaw to keep from blurting out that Micah wasn't the only person she would miss. Annoyed with herself over that truth, she went to gather her laptop bag and purse.

Joel placed a hand on her arm. "I'm a man of my word. I'll still accompany you, if you want."

Her heart lightened. She welcomed the idea, though she would grate her tongue before telling him that. So she kept it cool. "If you don't mind... It's only one more wedding, and then you'll be free of me."

His voice dropped, and he tucked a finger under her chin. "Sienna King, the last thing I want is to be free of you."

His words made her heart skip a beat, but she knew better than to read more into what Joel was saying. He loved words, made money writing them, so it was best to ignore anything that sounded too much like flirting. Sienna gave him a nervous chuckle and waved a hand.

"I find I've come to value our friendship, and being escorted by you will keep the men away."

He whipped his arms from left to right. "I'll come with my wing man."

As always, Sienna had a great comeback: "I'd prefer it if you come with a proper suit."

"I will."

She loitered for a second but could think of nothing else to say. And no good reason to stay. With a sigh, she strutted to the door. Joel accompanied her to her car. She rolled down her window and tossed out, "I'll see you tomorrow." When she realized what she'd said, a tsunami of sadness descended over her. "I forgot… There's no need for me to come." Sienna curved her shoulders and rested her head on the steering wheel.

"I'll see you this weekend." Joel's voice sounded sad and heavy, but Sienna couldn't meet his gaze. If she did, she would break down again, and she had to get home.

She straightened but didn't dare look his way. Instead, she whispered, "See you then," before pressing the gas.

Joel jumped awake. Micah. He hadn't heard Micah cry through the night, or he'd slept through it. He glanced at the clock and saw that it was 5:18 a.m. Turning on the bedside lamp, he felt his eyes go wide at the empty space beside the bed. How had he missed Micah's bellows? He patted the cool, untouched sheet and popped out of bed, turning his head to the left to check the bassinet. Only it wasn't there. His heart thumped as he sprinted toward the nursery, but Micah wasn't in there. Please don't let it be that Joel had been so tired that he had left Micah downstairs in the swing—or worse, on the couch. He was too young to roll over, but one couldn't risk it. Images of Micah lying helpless on the floor propelled Joel down the stairs.

Hopefully, Micah had slept through the night... *Wait.* He paused. Something wasn't right. The house felt... quiet. His brain struggled through the sleep fog to help him recall.

Halfway down the stairs, the memory hit him, and his chest felt like it was caving in. He doubled over, feeling relief pump through his veins, followed by a heavy rush of sadness. His knees buckled, and he sat on the steps.

His shoulders sagged. That's right—Micah wasn't there. Micah had left yesterday with Greg. His brother had called at midnight to say he had made it back to Louisiana without incident. Joel must have fallen asleep after that.

Holding on to the rail, Joel stood and made his way back upstairs. He slumped on his bed and bent over, cupping his head with his hands.

He missed Micah. And if he was feeling that way, he could guarantee that Sienna was up as well. Joel showered and dressed in his usual pair of jeans and a T-shirt before grabbing his keys and rushing out the door. He stopped at the bakery for the morning paper, apple fritters and cinnamon rolls before driving to Sienna's house.

He parked next to her vehicle, traipsed up the stairs to the second floor and then rapped on her door.

Seconds later, the door swung open.

"I knew you'd come." She eyed the brown paper bag and pointed. "I hope you brought some good stuff."

"I brought the biggest, softest apple fritters and cinnamon rolls I could find. Two of each."

She stepped aside to let him enter her apartment. "I already made some hot chocolate."

Unlike Joel, Sienna was still in her pajamas. Her eyes were red, her voice hoarse and her hair… Half her hair was out of the braids, her curls sticking upward. His mouth dropped. Joel couldn't think of a time he had seen Sienna without her hair perfect.

Wisdom declared that he keep his mouth shut, but this was Joel with Sienna. "You look like how I feel."

Sienna touched her head, not the least bit self-conscious. "I couldn't sleep. Figured I'd get a head start on taking these braids out before my hair appointment. Planning a new hairdo for the next wedding. Not sure yet."

"I'm sure whatever you do will be fabulous," he tossed out, his mind already on eating.

He placed the bag of goodies and the paper on the counter before retrieving two small plates. Seeing two steaming mugs of hot cocoa warmed his heart. After choosing the one with slightly less liquid, he took a sip.

Sienna came over and tore open the brown paper bag and took out a cinnamon roll. Taking a big bite, Sienna closed her eyes and moaned before licking icing off her lips. "Mmm… This is just what I needed."

They gathered the newspaper, the treats and the hot beverages and went to sit across from each other at the table. There was a pacifier and a bottle in the center, on top of the place mats.

Picking up the pacifier and holding it with his thumb and index finger, Joel said, "I miss him."

Sienna fussed with her pajama top. "Me too. I don't know what to do with myself. It's amazing how much he filled my day these past few weeks."

He drummed his fingers on the table. "Though it hurts, I have no regrets. I'd do it again in a heartbeat."

"Even though I cried my eyes out again when I got home last night, I feel the same." She let out a dramatic sigh. "I'm not one for wallowing in self-pity, but he's going to be a hard one to shake."

Joel's cell phone rang. It was his brother, calling on FaceTime. Scooting closer to Sienna, Joel answered. His brother's and Tessa's smiling faces appeared. Seeing their shining eyes eased Joel's heart.

"Hey, bro. We just wanted to tell you again how much we appreciate you taking care of Micah for us." Then Greg's brows shot up. "Great, Sienna is there too."

"Hi, Sienna! Thanks for being a stand-in mother to my son," Tessa said.

Sienna gave her a little wave before dabbing at her eyes. "It was my honor." Her voice wobbled. Joel grabbed a napkin from the table and pushed it in her hand. She whispered a thank-you before saying, "We're just glad you're okay."

"So somebody wanted to see you and say hello," Greg said.

Joel's lips widened into a smile when his brother turned the camera toward Micah. His heart melted when he saw that little face. Sienna shifted closer, her hand cupping his as she held the other side of the small screen. Seeing their hands joined made his insides crackle.

"Hey, Micah," she cooed, her eyes alight with joy.

"Hey, little man," Joel said. "I bet you slept well last night."

"Of course he did. He was with Mommy and Daddy." Sienna waved. "We love you, Micah."

This was the second time Sienna used *we* instead of *I*. Speaking for the both of them meant she had to see them as a unit, friends who shared the same attachment with his nephew.

So he took the liberty of saying, "We'll come see you soon."

Sienna tensed, and he heard a sharp intake of breath. Then: "Yes, we will."

His brother and wife were delighted, telling him they had more than enough room to accommodate them. They ended the call soon after that, and Joel placed the cell phone on the table.

Sienna's eyes connected with his. He wondered if she was going to fuss with him for committing her to go on a trip without discussing it with her first.

"That was really thoughtful of them to do. Seeing Micah's face made my day." Her voice sounded light and airy. "I think suggesting a visit was a good idea. I'm glad you thought of that, because it put things into perspective for me. Micah isn't gone forever—he's just in another state."

Looking into her eyes, Joel nodded. "Yeah, but it's a thousand miles away."

"Hours by plane..."

"Yeah. It's all about perspective." Joel glanced out the window, and the brightness of the sun lifted his spirits even further. Gaining confidence, he dared to reach over to take Sienna's hand in his. "I know I'm seeing you in a much different light this summer."

She lowered her eyes and brushed at her pajama pants. “How so?”

“I feel like we’re finally friends, and I have Micah to thank for that.” He cocked his head. “Do you feel the same?”

Joel turned so his legs touched hers; he was relieved when she didn’t pull away. He reached his hand up to touch her cheek. She was soft and smooth.

“Yes.” Her voice sounded breathy, but she didn’t look away.

Joel leaned forward, closer…

“What are we doing?” Sienna asked in a jerky voice, pulling back. Her eyes were wide with fear. “I don’t know if we should venture into something that could get awkward.”

Joel dropped his hand and swallowed. “Are you saying you don’t want to kiss me?”

“No, I do. I just don’t think it’s a good idea. It took us about twenty-four years to find our way to friendship. I don’t want to ruin that. Especially since I don’t know if this is all because of the emotions we’re experiencing over Micah’s departure.” She bit her lower lip, her eyes pleading with him to understand.

His shoulders slumped. “You’re right.” Then he raked a hand through his hair. “I value our friendship too much to put it at risk.”

“Ugh. I’m all confused.” She broke eye contact and picked up the newspaper. “This is new and exciting… But we’ve been pretend-dating and caring for Micah as parents. Those two factors are enough to muddy the waters and lull us into wanting things that aren’t based on something real.”

"I get it. Your logic makes sense." He then asked the question that made his heart hammer in his chest: "How about we attend this wedding as real dates instead of pretending?"

"I'd like that." Her lashes fluttered down toward her cheeks. "I think that's a good idea."

Sienna acting all shy made his lips quirk. It was adorable and made him want to kiss her even more. "Great. I'm looking forward to the weekend even more now." His hand grazed his five-o'clock shadow. He would call the barber to set an appointment.

Then she straightened. "I think a date would be a good first step in seeing if there could be something more… Either way, I want to preserve our friendship."

"I do as well." He grinned and then confessed, "I haven't been on a date in years. I hope I remember what to do."

"Me either." She touched her hair, and her mouth dropped. "But I do know that you better bring your A game."

"Challenge accepted." Joel made a mental note to buy a new suit before the weekend.

She gave him a soft smile. "I'm glad my first venture out in the dating world will be with you." Then she unfolded the newspaper. What she saw made her gasp. She placed a hand on her chest. "You didn't tell me I would be front-page news!"

Chapter Seventeen

"Thank you, Sienna. You're a lifesaver." Kelsey eased into the couch in her living room and bit into the watermelon before releasing a groan. "This is so good."

"It's not a problem, especially since you had perfect timing. I had just finished doing my hair."

After Joel had left for work, Sienna took out the rest of her braids and washed her hair. Just as she had been applying conditioner, Kelsey texted to ask if Sienna could pick up watermelon and strawberries since Zach had taken Mia and Morgan to the beach for the day.

In addition to purchasing enough fruit for herself and Kelsey, Sienna had bought Kelsey five-dollar flip-flops.

"How are you doing with Micah gone?" Kelsey asked, biting into a strawberry. Sienna had texted in the group chat yesterday, telling Kelsey and Jade about Micah's departure before continuing her crying fest.

"I'm doing okay." She ran a hand along her stone-washed jeans and dropped her gossip before eating some of her fruit. "Joel and I are going to the wedding as real dates this weekend."

That revelation caused Kelsey to drop her watermelon. Fortunately, it landed on her baby bump. "That's some serious tea you just spilled. What happened to going from hello to honeymoon?" She popped the watermelon into her mouth.

"Well, I was so used to telling Joel goodbye that I need time to get to hello." She took a delicious bite of strawberry. "And I don't know where he is in his relationship with God. I can't have a long-term relationship with someone who doesn't feel the same way about God that I do. There's a lot to unpack and discover, so I'm all about taking it slow, you know? See where it goes."

Kelsey nodded. "Understood. Does Joel know how you feel about dating?"

"What do you mean?"

Kelsey turned to her side, facing Sienna. "You've said many times you believe in dating only if there's a possibility of marriage. Otherwise, what's the point?"

"Of course I—I didn't tell him that." She let out a little laugh, feeling uneasy. "I didn't want to scare him. Or *me*, for that matter." Sienna rubbed her forehead. "We're navigating our way through feelings that I'm not sure are authentic or if they're linked to our love for Micah. So, like I said, we need time to process and see..."

"Hmm." Kelsey cocked her head. "This is new for you. The Sienna I know likes to know where she's heading before even starting the journey."

"Yeah, well. I'm trying something new with Joel. It's filled with uncertainty but also anticipation."

Her friend smiled. "We'll put this up as our number two prayer-list item. Number one being my delivery, of course."

"Agreed."

Lifting a brow, Kelsey snorted. "You and Joel? I tell you, I didn't see that one coming. God has a sense of humor. I can't wait for Jade to hear this new development."

Sienna tossed a strawberry at her friend. "I know she's going to have a field day at my expense." Glancing at her watch, she slapped her leg. "Let me get on to my hair appointment before I get charged a late fee."

On her way to the hair salon, Sienna thought about Kelsey's question about deviating from her position on dating. To some, it might seem archaic and even unrealistic, but Sienna hadn't expected she would want to date anyone. Before this summer, her computer had been her partner when she wasn't with her friends or involved with the church camp and activities. But she was allowed to change her mind. Wasn't she?

And Micah had been the catalyst for that change. He was the reason she and Joel had morphed from enemies into friends. Right as she pulled into the parking lot, Sienna remembered that she hadn't spoken to her mother since yesterday.

Seeing that she was ten minutes early, Sienna decided to FaceTime her mother. Just as she was about to hang up, Daphne picked up the call.

"Hey, Mom, how did your appointment go?" Sienna was pleased to note that Daphne appeared to have embraced her short hairdo. It looked like she had applied gel, and there were already tiny curls framing her face.

"It went well. I liked Dr. Yang. She placed me on a green diet to give me a cleansing, and we've met virtually each evening to check in."

Then Daphne squinted. "Your eyes look puffy. Are you alright?"

The caring in her mother's voice almost made her unravel. She fanned her face. "I'm good. I'm about to get my hair done so I'm ready for the wedding I have to attend this weekend."

"And how's that precious baby doing?"

Her smile slipped. "He went home yesterday."

"Oh, that explains why you look like you've lost your kitten." Daphne placed a hand over her mouth.

"I wouldn't know, since you wouldn't let me have a pet when I was younger. I'm sad, but at the same time, I'm happy that Tessa—that's Micah's mother—is okay. So I'm happy but also sad at the same time. But after being with him, I know I want to be a mother for sure." Adjusting her iPhone on the steering wheel column, Sienna then told her mother about her real date with Joel. Which of course meant she had to divulge that they had been pretend dating, something her mother found fascinating.

Her mother's eyes twinkled. "I can't wait for you to declare your undying love and get your happy-ever-after ending." She sighed. "I can't wait to have grandchildren to spoil."

"Whoa," Sienna sputtered. "You're getting ahead of yourself. No one said anything about being in love." She placed a hand on her chest. "Since when did you become such a romantic?"

"Since I started binge-watching romance movies." She lifted up three fingers. "Right now, you and Joel are in the third act. There's only one pivotal scene left, and I hope you two hurry and get to it."

Sienna held up her index finger. “Slow down. I have a major concern. I need to know where Joel stands with God. He comes to church for special occasions or if he’s writing an article for the town paper, but that doesn’t mean he has a solid relationship with God. I just have to find out where he’s at, and that’s why I’m moving slow.”

“There you go, sounding all stuffy and preachy again. An attitude like that will keep you single for life.” Her mother rolled her eyes. “All you need is a good man, and Joel is a good man. Your father likes him, and we think Joel complements you. He can deal with your sass.”

Sienna disagreed. “There are plenty of good men in the world. I must be with someone who has a strong foundation and faith so we can be a source of encouragement to each other. It’s important to me. And yes, I will remain single rather than deal with the headache of being with someone of unequal faith.”

On the inside, she groaned. How she wished her parents understood what her faith meant to her. They didn’t get how tough it had been growing up with doubts about being in love and with fears of being accepted. If Jade hadn’t invited her to church and she hadn’t heard how much God loved and accepted her, Sienna didn’t know what kind of trouble she would have gotten caught up in. But God. That’s why she couldn’t let Him go. Her parents put all her successes on their good parenting. Not on God. However, Sienna knew better. But she wasn’t about to revisit that fifteen-year-old argument with her mother.

“All right. All right. Let’s agree to disagree,” Daphne

said. "Now, back to the good part. What are you going to wear?"

"I already bought my dress," Sienna said. "It's a cocktail flare dress with pockets. I think it's cute."

"Cute won't cut it. You need to wow him with your curves."

Sienna chuckled. "I don't think there's any hiding those, but I'll let you know how things go with Joel." Her mother waved and disconnected. Sienna gathered her purse and walked into the hair salon, appreciating the blast of the air conditioner when she entered the building.

Layla, the stylist, greeted her and gestured for Sienna to take a seat in the black swivel chair. She swung her around, and Sienna's mouth dropped when she saw her hair in the mirror. "The humidity has not been kind. I look like a character in *The Lion King*."

Picking up her comb, Layla asked, "Are you getting your usual braids again?"

"How about we go with a new color and a twist out? That should last about two weeks."

Layla's brows rose. She went to retrieve her color swatches. "Something new—I like that."

Yes, she was looking forward to something new too. And Sienna was brimming with so much excitement, she couldn't wait to see Joel again. She couldn't wait to see how things developed.

Joel was scared to see Sienna. Their conversation that morning had raised his anxiety levels to epic proportions. At first, he had been looking forward to taking their friendship to dating, but then he had started thinking about Sienna—the woman.

And Joel knew he fell short.

She was on the top floor and he was in the basement, and the journey to the top was a long one.

Women like Sienna weren't about keeping things casual, no matter what they said. Sienna was a spicy cactus on the outside, but on the inside, she was a delicate flower. Dating someone like her came with expectations. Like marriage. Frankly, Joel didn't see himself donning a tuxedo again and waiting for a bride who might never appear.

Maybe he should leave well enough alone.

But then he would miss his chance with Sienna. He admired her sass, her tenacity and the way she cared for his nephew. He liked being in her presence, but her warning that this could be a phase, a reaction to Micah's leaving, echoed in his mind. He couldn't use Sienna as a substitute for Micah or to fill his loneliness.

That's why he was now sitting across from August in his office at Millennial House of Praise. Joel had reached out to the pastor, who was the closest thing he had to a confidant and friend, to see if he was available for a heart-to-heart. To help him make sense of his jumbled mind.

August was only a year or two older than Joel, and he was also single. But he wasn't discontented like Joel. That was something Joel admired about him, and it encouraged him to seek his advice on many occasions. None before had held this much importance, though.

"What's going on?" August said, easing back into his leather chair.

Joel squared his shoulders. "Sienna and I are going

on a date." Then he exhaled, sat back in his chair and folded his arms.

August waited a beat before he must have realized Joel expected him to say something. He gestured. "And..."

"'And'?" Joel's brows furrowed. "That's massive. You know it's no secret how we feel—*used* to feel—about each other. I hate to bring up the church picnic a few years back, but I'm pretty sure your ears are still ringing from our big blowout. I would think you would be shocked."

"Okay, you've explained how you think I should feel. But what really matters here is, what do *you* think about it?"

Joel rubbed his chin. "My emotions are like a seesaw right now. I feel elated, but I'm terrified. I don't deserve a woman like Sienna. She's smart, she's got spunk and I'm just...me."

"Sienna is one of my most devoted volunteers here at the church. I never have to wonder about her follow-through." He gave Joel a calculating glance. "But then again, so are you. You're consistent, determined—and when you're after a story, you're tenacious." August looked upward. "Actually, the more I think about it, the more I see the potential between you both."

Joel's fear lessened. Somewhat. "But, uh, she's more connected to God than I am. Than I ever will be." Joel coughed, embarrassed to admit that to a man of God. He tensed, waiting for the fiery reproach. But there was none.

"Why is that a problem?" August asked.

His tongue loosened. "I don't pray often, and I couldn't find any of the books in the Bible without an index. In short, as you church folks would say, I'm not worthy."

"Good. I'm glad you realize that." August rested his hands on the oak table. "None of us are worthy or will ever be worthy. That's why we rely on God to do all the heavy lifting."

"Maybe God did that for you, but He didn't for me." The pastor's brows rose at Joel's bitter words, so Joel continued. "Where was He when my father bullied my mother? They would be in church, smiling, and then hours later, he would abuse her. Why did God allow that?" The hurt poured out of him then. "And when I protested, my father turned on me. He forced my mother and brother to choose sides. Neither had anything to do with me."

Joel's voice cracked, and the tears slid down his cheeks. August went to get Joel a bottle of water from the mini fridge he kept in his office. After thanking him, Joel took a few sips and cleared his throat. "I'm sorry. I don't know where that all came from." He lowered his head. He was supposed to be talking about Sienna, not his past. That was a sea full of self-pity, and he was content to remain on the shore of his life—yet here he was, diving in.

"Your past is important. It's a part of who you are." August opened the top drawer of his desk and crooked his finger at Joel. "Want a snack?"

Joel stood and bent over to take a peek. Then he gasped. There were chocolate bars, mints, cookies, chips and all sorts of goodies. He had no idea August was a secret snacker, but it did explain his slight paunch. The reporter in him had questions. Maybe this was his way of dealing with the stress of his profession. But Joel swallowed his curiosity. Joel chose a granola bar and returned to his seat. August grabbed a Moon Pie.

The pastor leaned forward and clasped his hands. “God has been there with you through everything you’ve been through in your life. Nothing that has happened to you was an accident. In fact, it was all a part of His divine plan to bring you here to this moment, and possibly to Him.”

“Wow,” Joel said. “You’re giving me a lot to think about. But what about Sienna?” He was eager to hear what August felt about that.

“God can only do so much. That’s for you to figure out,” August said. “You have to decide if she’s who you want and whether or not you’re going to allow your past experiences to prevent you from getting what should be yours.” Was Sienna truly meant to be his, though? That’s the question Joel asked himself after leaving August’s office. His heart screamed yes. And he was open to exploring that possibility, which meant he had some soul-searching to do before the wedding. Because with a woman like Sienna, you had to be *sure* sure. If he wanted her—nope, there were no ifs—since he knew he wanted her in his life, he had to come correct.

Like August said, he had to make a decision. He could only pray that he would make the right one for himself. And Sienna.

Chapter Eighteen

For some reason Joel had been avoiding her all week. He had answered her texts, but when she called, he wouldn't answer, and when she would invite him for lunch or dinner, he declined, saying he was busy with work. Sienna stood before her bathroom mirror and admitted his behavior had her concerned.

She was a confident woman who knew she had a lot to offer, but Joel appeared to be pulling back, and that didn't sit well with her. She wrinkled her nose. Maybe she was being too pushy and he was too polite to say anything. Something she asked God about in her daily prayers. She was picky with the men she liked, and so just finding out that she gelled with Joel made her eager.

But this was one distance she couldn't swim alone. And now she wasn't sure Joel wanted to embark on this discovery with her.

That uncertainty didn't keep her from bringing out her A game for their date, though. Her curls popped, her makeup was flawless and her dress accentuated her figure. She knew Joel would find no fault with her physically.

But what if he was unsure of the woman underneath? That gave her pause.

Then her sass rescued her from feeling despondent. "If he's unsure, it's better you find out now." She pointed at the mirror. "And if you know what's good for you, you're going to ask him."

Satisfied, Sienna checked herself one last time before walking out of the bathroom.

The doorbell rang, and she looked at her watch. Joel was right on time. She headed toward the front door and promised to remain civil when she saw him. If the phrase *play it cool* were a T-shirt, it would have her face on it; that's how cool she would be. Then she opened the door.

Joel had gotten a haircut. His locks had been faded and his beard outlined. And he was dressed in a two-piece navy suit with a white shirt and black tie. She noted that this suit appeared to be tailor-made for him.

"You look amazing," she said. "To say you clean up well would be an understatement."

In return, he eyed her with appreciation, taking in her rust-colored dress. Once she saw his face, Sienna knew she had made the right decision.

"You, my dear, are breathtaking." Joel held out a bouquet of peach-colored roses. She thanked him and inhaled their fragrance before placing the flowers on her kitchen counter. However, before she could seek out a vase for them, Joel presented her with a corsage, which he placed on her left hand.

"You're definitely making up for my no-show prom

date," she said, touched by his gesture. "I love it." If this was anyone but Joel, she would have given him a peck on the cheek, but Sienna didn't trust herself to stop there. So she patted his arm instead.

"Wait. You got ghosted at prom?"

"That's a story for another time." Sienna grabbed her clutch and glanced at her watch. "If we leave now, we should be right on time." Both Jade and Kelsey would be in attendance as well. The wedding venue was at the church, and when they arrived, the parking lot was already full. It seemed like the whole town had received an invitation.

Though Joel offered to let her out in front, Sienna declined. She wanted to arrive with her date arm in arm. Joel reached into the back for a small plastic bag, but she didn't ask what was inside, thinking it was his camera.

When they entered the church, Sienna couldn't hold her gasp. The sanctuary had been transformed with dozens and dozens of white roses, which gave off the most wonderful aroma. She saw Zach, Kelsey and Jade waving from the pew three rows from the front, and she sauntered down the aisle to sit beside them.

"You guys look fabulous," she said to her friends and then sat, leaving room for Joel. Joel and Zach gave each other some dap, and Joel complimented her friends.

"So do you," Jade said, giving her a thumbs-up. "You're working that dress."

"Thanks." Sienna blushed.

Kelsey opened her large purse and pulled out a banana.

"You'd better not let August see you," Sienna warned.

Her friend shrugged. "This baby is hungry, and if I don't feed him, I won't be held responsible for what might happen." She peeled the banana and practically stuffed half of it in her mouth.

Jade pointed to Kelsey's protruding stomach. "She popped overnight, I'm telling you. Kelsey wasn't that big yesterday."

Kelsey was dressed in a baby doll dress with crystals embellishing the collar and a pair of fancy flip-flops. Sienna had found the bedazzled pair, which had extra cushion and support, online and had surprised Kelsey with the gift.

"He's almost done cooking." Kelsey patted her bump and finished the rest of the banana.

Sienna pursed her lips. "From where I'm sitting, I'd say you need to turn off the oven because that bird's about to burn."

Jade gave her a shove. "You're wrong about that."

"You're glowing," Joel broke in to offer. Then he reached into the plastic bag, pulled out two more corsages, similar to hers, and handed them to her friends.

"Aw." Jade's face melted. "That's so sweet of you." She slipped the corsage on her wrist.

"And thoughtful." Kelsey sniffled. "I'm sorry, this little bundle has turned me into a cry baby." Zach helped his wife put on her corsage.

Sienna pinned Joel with a stare just as the processional was about to start. "I had no idea. All this time I've known you, I didn't see the considerate man that you are. But I'm seeing you, Joel. I'm seeing you now."

Baby steps were still steps. He had acted on what was in his heart, and he hadn't been rejected. In fact, all three women had appreciated his gesture.

Having Sienna look at him in a way she hadn't before had also bolstered him. Joel had used the week to meet with August. It had been tough declining Sienna's offers to get together, but Joel had to make room in his life for God.

The funny thing was that the clearer Joel was on the path needed to take with God, the clearer his next steps with Sienna were. He had written examples of the ways in which he could show Sienna how he felt to build his trust that she could love him in return in his Notes app.

Because this much was clear: Joel was in love with the woman sitting next to him.

He told himself that several times every day, *I am in love with Sienna*, and he repeated it until he could express it as a statement of fact, until it was no longer about wondering how she was feeling. Because this love was very much about him and giving himself the opportunity to love, regardless of whether or not it was returned. As August had said, for as long as Joel had doubted how he felt about God, God had remained sure of how He felt about Joel.

That's the approach he would take with Sienna. He would chip away at her resolve one day at a time until he had her heart. Joel was a patient man. He reached for one of the church fans, wishing they would turn up the air conditioning.

When the bride walked down the aisle, Joel pictured Sienna doing the same one day, and he dared to hope that he would be the groom waiting at the altar. That image made him smile. His smile remained all through the vows. Just when the couple were about to kiss, Joel heard a loud gasp and an "Oh no." He turned to see what the commotion was all about.

Kelsey was covering her face and mumbling under her breath. Zach had jumped to his feet; they were drawing the attention of many others in the party. Then Joel noticed the puddle on the floor, and he knew exactly what was going on. Sienna and Jade sprang into action, scurrying with Kelsey toward the exit.

Joel grabbed Sienna's clutch, Jade's car keys and Zach's wallet and stuffed them into his plastic bag before quickly making his way out of the building. He figured Sienna had left with the others and they were now en route to the hospital.

When he saw Sienna standing there, Joel's love for her was magnified. Despite the fact that her best friend in the world was about to give birth, Sienna hadn't left. She had waited. For him. She yelled at him to quit stalling and that he wasn't moving fast enough as they dashed toward his Jeep, but Joel didn't care. She had waited.

That's what counted. And that meant something. It meant she cared about him too. And for the first time in a long time, Joel dared to hope.

Chapter Nineteen

Sienna's left eye ticked. When they arrived at the hospital, the press was camped outside. News traveled fast. Possibly because of the man sitting next to her. She gave Joel the side-eye. Kelsey's husband was a retired basketball player and had been the pastor of a megachurch in Philadelphia. She looked at Joel, who was busy trying to find parking. "Why did you do this?"

"I didn't," Joel said, popping a mint into his mouth and then offering one to her. "I'm insulted that you think I would do that."

"You were the last to come outside the church. Enough time to make a phone call or send a text." She opened the wrapper and bit off a small piece of the candy.

Joel sighed. "Sienna, I stayed behind to gather your purse, Jade's keys and Zach's wallet." He pointed to the back seat, where he had placed the plastic bag. "You can check it if you don't believe me." Then he muttered, "Not that I have a reason to lie."

She had forgotten to take her belongings when she rushed out of the church, so she needed to be thanking him instead of yelling at him. But Sienna pressed forward. “This is classic Joel—all about the story. Forget about who it hurts.”

“Look, I told you that it wasn’t me. Now leave it alone.”

Oh no, he didn’t take that tone with her. “Pull over and let me out.” Sienna pressed the lock button to unlock the door.

“I’m not going to do that,” Joel said, sounding exasperated. “Why don’t you quit accusing me of something I didn’t do and help me find a parking spot?”

She folded her arms. “Just let me out at the front.”

Joel swerved the Jeep out of the way of a car coming toward them. “Why are you trying to start an argument when we’ve been getting along so well? I feel like you’re purposely trying to ruin things between us. Like you’re rubbing together old sticks to kindle a fire no one wants started.”

Because she didn’t trust him. Or rather, she was afraid to trust him. However, Sienna couldn’t utter those words, because then he would see what was in her heart. Joel found an open spot and parked. Sienna hurried out of the vehicle, careful not to tap or dent the truck parked next to them. Then she started moving.

Joel caught up with her by the entrance. As hot as it was, he could see perspiration dotting her upper lip and forehead. “The press could be here for someone else. Did you even consider that?”

Her shoulders slumped. “I suppose you’re right. I’m sorry for coming at you without concrete proof. I’m just…frustrated.”

His eyes were gentle. “What’s wrong?”

"I keep waiting for you to tell me why you blew me off all week and then showed up handing me and my friends corsages and being all thoughtful. It's discombobulating."

"Oh, that's the bee in your bonnet." He smiled, touching her cheek. "When I wasn't at work, I was with August. I had some things to work out..." He cupped her face. "Things I have to deal with if I want to take our friendship to the next level."

She sucked in a breath. "'The next level'?" she squeaked out. For her, the next level meant marriage. For him, it could mean something entirely different. It could be all about a fleeting physical connection, not a lasting one.

He moved close. And closer. Then he nodded and said, "Yes," his minty breath on her face. Her heart rate escalated, and though they were outside, Sienna felt like she couldn't breathe.

"I think we have a few steps—no, make that a few escalator rides—until we get to that level you're talking about." She patted his chest. "We'd better get inside. Kelsey must be wondering where I am." She inched back. He inched forward.

His darkened eyes held intent. "The delivery could take hours."

Wow. He was messing with her equilibrium—in a good way. Sienna found she liked this assertive Joel. There was no guessing what was on his mind. He wanted to kiss her.

He grabbed her hand and led her through the sliding doors of the hospital and out of the scorching heat. Sienna struggled to keep up with his longer strides. He scanned the area and ducked behind a large shrub, pulling her into his hard chest.

Before she could catch her breath, Joel touched his lips to hers.

It was downright ridiculous that the most antagonizing woman in the world could also taste the sweetest. He couldn't wait to do it again.

Yet he knew that it would be some time before she allowed him the luxury. Their kiss had spooked her. After Joel had ended it, she rushed out of his arms and put distance between them.

Joel had watched her run, understanding why she had to flee. Even now, as they sat with Jade in the maternity waiting area, she stayed away from him. Every now and again, her glance would slide his way, but then she would break eye contact.

No words of love had been spoken. It wasn't the right place. It wasn't the right time. And for someone of her faith—and soon to be his—that wasn't enough. Attraction needed a solid foundation. Those had been August's exact words.

His greater concern now was his and Sienna's spiritual compatibility. She was far ahead of him in that race, and he didn't know how he would ever catch up, or be able to encourage her in the Word, when he had so much to learn. He felt inadequate in that department, and according to August, there was no crash course. The race wasn't for the swift; it was all about endurance. And patience. And steadfastness.

August had assured him that all God needed was

Joel's zeal, and then He would equip him to be the husband Sienna needed.

Yes, *husband*. Not boyfriend. Not friend.

Joel was ready to wait at the end of the aisle for this woman. He was willing to put his heart out there because she was worth it. And…so was he. When he told her he loved her, he would follow up by asking for her hand in marriage. Sienna had told him that her mother wanted her settled before she died, and Joel intended to grant that wish, if Sienna would have him. If Sienna loved him. If Sienna wanted to marry him. Some big *ifs*, but Joel had to take the risk.

Since Sienna was seated next to Jade and pretending to ignore him, Joel sent her a text. Can we talk?

He saw her look at her phone and wrinkle her nose. Not now, she texted back.

Then when?

She sent him a shrugging emoji and went back to her conversation with Jade.

Joel had stood to stretch his legs when his cell phone rang. It was Skip. Joel walked outside the room to answer the call.

"I'm glad I caught you. Listen, there's a developing story that, right now, is just hearsay. Have you heard of Daphne King?"

The name of his potential mother-in-law. "Y-yes. I have." Joel gripped the phone.

"She's a renowned harpist. This woman's been in movies, played for presidents—and she's one of Swallow's Creek's own. Daphne and her husband moved to Pittsburgh a year ago."

"Yes, I know all of this." Joel wished Skip would

get to the main point of his call so he could get back to waiting for Kelsey's baby to arrive.

"Well, I have it on good authority that she's dying. My source told me that Daphne King has a few months to live. I'd like you to do an exposé on her before she passes."

Joel's feet felt wooden. There was no way he would want to capitalize on Sienna's sorrow. "I—I can't do that."

"Why not?"

He lowered his voice to a whisper. "I'm sort of dating her daughter."

"Oh!" Skip paused. "Well, that's even better. You'll have the inside scoop, a front-row seat. All I would need you to do is take some photos, take a few notes. It could be anonymous. I can have one of the junior writers compose the actual article. Leave your name out of it completely."

Joel wiped his brow. He could almost see the salacious look on Skip's face and wondered how many times he himself had been that way. But the key words were *had been*—as in, not anymore. "I can't betray Daphne like that. Or her daughter. Capitalizing on someone else's illness doesn't sit well with me."

"A story is a story," Skip said. "And if you want to be editor in chief, you have to do things that are not always pleasant."

Joel's jaw clenched. "Listen, I've been jumping through hoops for you these past few months, and I'm done jumping."

Skip pressed on, disregarding Joel's words. "Think about it. I'll be in touch." Then he ended the call.

As far as Joel was concerned, there was no need to think about something he knew he would never do. For a second, Joel panicked at the thought of losing that promotion and having to see the editor in chief position go to someone else. But integrity and love won out. Joel realized that he would rather be denied a job for doing what was right than granted one for doing what was wrong.

Chapter Twenty

Seated at her kitchen table, Sienna expelled a huge yawn. Though she had enjoyed being at the hospital for the countdown until baby Aiden's appearance, she was both thrilled and exhausted. Both mom and baby were doing well. Seeing Aiden's face had made her miss Micah even more.

If he was here, she would be about ready to head over to Joel's house. If she was struggling like this, Sienna knew Joel was too. There was no going back to normal for either of them. Knowing she wouldn't go back to sleep, Sienna decided to work on her dissertation presentation.

Her doorbell rang.

"It's open," Sienna shouted, knowing it would only be one person at this hour.

Joel came in, holding a bag she guessed contained bagels. Then he locked the door behind him. "I know this is a safe town—but these days, you can never be too careful."

"I just unlocked it a few minutes ago, but you're right. I'll be more cautious." Another yawn escaped.

Goodness, she was sleepy. From her peripheral vision, she noticed that Joel hadn't moved from where he was.

She glanced over to see him clutching his chest, and she arched her brow.

"I'm in shock that you gave in so easily." Joel chuckled, setting the bag on the counter. He washed his hands and then placed a couple of bagels—cinnamon-raisin for her and blueberry for him—in the toaster and opened the refrigerator to search for the whipped cream cheese. "I bought some orange tea leaves that I want us to try." Once he had found the container, Joel gathered two plates, a knife and two mugs before putting on some hot water. "What are you up to?"

"I'm supposed to be practicing my presentation but my brain is too tired to cooperate." She yawned again and rested her head in her hands. "I can't flub this." The other reason why Sienna was so loopy was because she kept replaying their kiss in her head. She dragged her mind back to the conversation. "Right after I hand in these revisions, I'm going to reward myself by sleeping for at least twelve hours."

The toaster popped and Joel picked up the hot bagels with his thumb and index finger before tossing them on the plate. "Whew. Those are hot."

After he placed their breakfast before them, Joel pulled out a chair and rubbed his hands. "How can I help?"

Her brows rose. "You want to help?" She took a dainty bite of her bagel.

"Yeah. I took a day off to recuperate after yesterday's excitement. I had less than four hours of sleep, but I'm ahead on my assignments."

Yet he had shown up with food and was volunteering to help her. Her heart warmed. "Thanks for sharing your day off with me." She lowered her lashes. "It means a lot."

They dug in to their meal.

Joel wiped his mouth. "So how's your mother doing?"

"She's doing good, actually. For the first time since this whole ordeal, Mom felt optimistic. She seemed hopeful to work with Dr. Yang."

"That's good to hear. Real good." He took one last big bite of his bagel. "Pull up that presentation." His mouth was stuffed, but she was able to understand his garbled words.

Sienna shifted her laptop so he could see, cleared her throat and then began. Then, over the next few hours, Joel offered her suggestions that tightened up her presentation until Sienna felt she was more than ready.

Her eyes widened when she saw it was almost midday. "Whew. I had no idea it was so late." She sent her final presentation to the committee, stood, stretched and then went to get a glass of water.

"Are you hungry?" she asked. On cue, her stomach growled. She wandered over to the drawer where she stored takeout menus. "Are you in the mood for Chinese? My treat."

"I'm not picky," Joel said before tossing out, "How about we go out to eat instead? There's a place near the outskirts of town with some good old-fashioned soul food."

"That sounds good, but it will still be my treat. Give me five minutes to change." When Joel didn't argue, Sienna put away the menus, then donned a dress and sandals. Next, she brushed her hair in a bun and applied edge gel so not even a single strand was out of place. Finally, she put on some coral lipstick.

Draping her purse across her body, Sienna strutted back to the living area. "Thanks for your assistance today. You were a great help."

Joel puffed out his chest. "I'm glad to hear that. I plan to be all you need from now on."

She placed a hand over her heart. "Strong words." The now-familiar tension rose between them.

He stood. "I plan to back it up. That's a promise."

Sienna released a breath of air. Joel was…intense. He got out of his seat and came over to stand close to her. Close enough for her to pick up the scent of his signature cologne. Throughout that morning, Joel had invented reasons to make physical contact, making her very aware of his presence.

"I'm seeking someone who motivates me to be more. Someone who challenges me and who won't let me sweet-talk my way out of anything." He snaked his hand around her neck. "Someone like you, Sienna King."

Her breath caught. Talk about saying the right things. "What do you want from me?"

"Simply put, I want you for my wife."

She gasped. *Wife?* "You just jumped over the *I love you* and the dating phase to talk of marriage?"

Joel hugged her. "When you know, you know."

Those words made her lose her breath. She moved out of his arms. "We can continue this discussion after we've eaten."

"All right. I'll take the fact that you didn't shut me down as a good sign."

She rolled her eyes. "It's more like, I'm too hungry to argue. Let's go." Since he couldn't see her, she dared to smile. Sienna was secretly pleased Joel was talking about marriage instead of dating. It meant his focus was on the long-term, something permanent. It meant Joel understood he was dealing with a diamond. God's girl. First class.

Just as they got into his Jeep, Joel's phone pinged. He scanned the text, grunted and tossed his phone in the console. Then he began to mutter to himself. Sienna's curiosity inflated like a balloon. "Something wrong?"

He waved a hand. "Naw. Nothing I can't handle." Though the muscles in his jaw were working overtime.

"I'm happy to be your sounding board. You've done the same for me."

His phone rang loudly in the small space. Sienna deduced it might be the same person who'd texted him, because Joel's face twisted. But he answered.

"Hey, Skip," Joel said, mouthing that it was his boss and turning down the volume.

She fanned herself with a hand so Joel would get the AC going. Sweat beads were already lining her forehead from the heat. He started up the Jeep.

Skip's voice was clear and loud in the cab. "Listen, I need to know if you've sweetened up that girlfriend of yours yet."

Sienna frowned. Was Joel going around town, telling people she was his girlfriend? Someone was getting ahead of himself. One kiss did not a girlfriend make.

Joel gave her a guilty look before he shifted the call to his cell phone and pressed his phone to his ear.

Sienna didn't even try to pretend she wasn't eavesdropping. In fact, she scooted over and cocked her head.

Joel's heart thumped in his chest. He wasn't about to exit the Jeep and make Sienna more suspicious. Although, knowing Sienna, she would follow him. "Skip, why are you calling me on my day off?"

"There's no such thing when you're editor in chief," Skip countered. His voice carried through the line. "Now, I need to know when you'll have that exposé on Daphne King, because I want this story before the national news picks it up."

Judging by Sienna's sharp intake of breath, Joel knew he was going to have to do some serious explaining. "I already told you how I felt about that."

It was as if he hadn't spoken. "You have two days, and then I expect to see the story in my inbox." Skip ended the call.

Joel faced Sienna, hating the mistrust in her flashing eyes. "That wasn't what it sounded like."

"Oh really? Because it sounded like you're doing an exposé on my dying mother for the sake of national exposure." Her voice cracked. "Never mind that this is the most difficult time in all our lives. I can't believe you would agree to that."

"I didn't—"

She interrupted him. "You were real slick with it too. Coming here under the pretense of helping me with my dissertation so you could probe into my mother's condition." Her eyes held hurt. "I bought it too."

"I wish you would give me a chance to explain," he

pleaded. "It feels like you've been waiting for the proverbial shoe to drop."

"Give you a chance? You want me to *give you a chance* to continue taking advantage of me?"

Joel's frustration increased, along with his anger. "I thought we were at a place in our relationship where you would give me the benefit of the doubt to hear me out. But you've already judged me. Just like you did at the hospital."

"I apologized for that," she said, holding up an index finger. "But let's not confuse that incident with this one. I clearly heard your boss say he expects to get that article in two days."

Joel counted to three. "I wasn't going to do the article, Sienna."

She scoffed. "Yeah, right. You're too ambitious to turn down the chance to have your article go viral." Her eyes filled. "You're exactly who I thought you were all these years, and I feel foolish for trusting you, for falling…" She unlocked the door. "I'm getting out of here."

The pain in her voice was his undoing, so Joel didn't try to stop her. He watched her retreating frame, his heart breaking.

Joel had tried to show through his actions how he felt about Sienna by helping her achieve the thing she most desired, and it hadn't been good enough. She would never see him in a positive light. Without trust and communication, a relationship—much less a marriage—would fail.

It wasn't in his nature to give up easily, but falling in love had made him insecure and unsure of how to advocate for himself. His heart ached at the disappointment etched on her face and the tears pooled in her eyes. He hadn't been able to please his parents; why had he ever expected to please her?

The sky cracked. A drop of rain hit his windshield.

Her distrust of him cut him to the core and inflicted damage to his pride. Though he loved her, Joel knew he couldn't spend the rest of his life with someone who wouldn't stand by his side at the mere hint of a challenge. But…

He drummed his fingers on the steering wheel. But he was in love with this woman, and as August had told him, love was a choice. A commitment.

The droplets turned into rain. Sienna was now about to step inside the house.

No way sitting there was the right move. Not for him. Joel opened the door and bounded out of the vehicle. "Sienna, I love you!" he yelled at the top of his lungs, sprinting up the steps. The stubborn woman dashed inside, closing the door. Joel banged on her door, calling for her even as the rain pelted his skin, plastering his hair to his face, making it difficult for him to speak.

Still, he yelled until he was hoarse.

Twenty minutes later, he reentered his car, soaked, dejected and resolved. This was the last time he would put himself out there for a woman. First, Elizabeth—and now Sienna. Maybe love wasn't in God's plan for him.

Chapter Twenty-One

I messed up. Sienna sat on her couch and texted the Three Amigas group chat. I messed up real bad. It was hard for her to admit defeat, but this was one war she had lost and would lose time and time again.

Oh no!! What happened??? Jade responded first.

Kelsey chimed in next. I thought you said you were ready to go.

Sienna couldn't hold in her tears. She had held it together throughout her dissertation defense—which she'd passed—but it was like her heart had run out of gas and she lacked the strength to go farther. Because she didn't answer, Jade video-called the group chat.

Wiping her face, Sienna answered, careful not to smudge the screen. Both Kelsey and Jade were on. She drew a breath and said, "I miss Joel." There. She had spoken the words aloud. Sienna fell back into the chair, relieved but also tense, waiting for her friends' reactions.

"Say what?" Jade boomed out.

Sienna sniffled. "I caught the love bug, and it's been dragging me down these past ten days."

Kelsey was silent before she finally addressed Jade. "I *told you* she was lovesick." She looked into the camera. "What happened between you two?"

Sienna rushed out a quick explanation about what Joel's boss was forcing him to do. She told them about Joel shouting out how he loved her and how she had refused to open the door and everything up until he had left.

"Have you reached out?" Kelsey asked.

Sienna shook her head. "I don't know what to say to him."

"You just don't want to admit that you were wrong for what you did," Jade shot back.

"It's more than that," Sienna whispered. "I'm scared."

"What are you scared of?" Kelsey asked.

"I feel like I'm a neon sign with the words *I love Joel* on my forehead."

Kelsey's eyes softened. "But he feels the same way about you."

Sienna tried to explain. "I don't want to be anyone's yo-yo. That's how it's always been with my parents..."

"But not with us." Kelsey's comment settled into Sienna's heart. She was sure of her place with her friends, which made her free to be herself. Just as she was free to be herself with Joel. In fact, he liked her sass, her spirit, and he wasn't seeking to squelch it.

"Ugh. Please don't tell me that's why you missed the sports day. I had to scramble to find a judge after you backed out."

"I had to. I couldn't face him."

Jade huffed. "Joel wasn't even there. I think he went to see his brother in Louisiana."

Kelsey adjusted Aiden so all Sienna could see was the top of his little head. That made her miss Micah. And Joel had gone to see Micah. Without her. Anger blazed, and she welcomed it. It was better than sitting in the self-pity party.

"I can't believe he would go see Micah and not tell me. He did that to spite me."

Jade looked at Sienna as if she were bananas. "Are you for real? You have no right getting upset when you shut him out."

"Maybe he's as heartbroken as you are and needs to be around family, just as you are reaching out to your friends right now," Kelsey offered.

"Maybe..." Sienna's chin wobbled. "I didn't know love would feel like this—so gut-wrenching. I should have never let him go."

"He's not dead," Jade shot out.

The friends broke into laughter, which lightened the mood.

"You're right. I'm making this way more dramatic than it has to be."

Kelsey chuckled. "But isn't that you? You always have to be extra."

Jade wagged a finger. "Now, promise us that you'll call the man and put him, you and us out of our misery. Because if you're miserable, we're all miserable."

"I will."

The doorbell rang, and Sienna ended the call with her friends to see who was at her door. Her heart pounded, wondering if it was Joel. Her eyes went wide when she saw who was outside.

"Give me one second," she yelled before skittering

into her bathroom to wash her face and apply foundation on her face. She scrutinized her red eyes, then shrugged. Hopefully, that could be attributed to allergies. Whatever. She couldn't do anything about it now.

Dashing back to the door, Sienna opened the door and stepped back to welcome her parents inside. As she had with her friends, Sienna had urged her parents to watch the defense virtually, just in case. So she was surprised to see they had made the five-hour trek to Delaware.

The minute her mother passed the threshold, she grabbed Sienna in her arms. "I'm sorry, honey."

Sienna returned the hug, caught off guard by her mother's display of affection. "What are you sorry about? I'm now Dr. King, just like you've always wanted. I thought you'd be pleased."

Neither parent responded at first, which was weird. Instead, they gave each other an awkward look before her father held out his arms. Okay, she was confused, but she would go with it. She stepped into his arms, closed her eyes, welcoming the feel of his strong arms around her.

Lennox gave her a pat on the back. "That's not it. We're proud of you, honey."

She felt like a caterpillar in a cocoon and snuggled into his chest before she remembered she was now a butterfly. So she broke free and folded her arms. "What's this about?" She looked between both her parents and raised her brows. Then a thought occurred.

She whipped to face her mom. "Please tell me you're…maintaining." Odd choice of words, but Sienna didn't want to ask outright if her mother had gotten worse. She scanned her mother from head to toe. Daphne looked…well. Her cheeks had good color—and in fact, her mother looked like her old self. Even her tiny curls had a luster to them.

Daphne wrung her hands before bidding Sienna to follow them to sit on her couch. "We realize we may have steered you wrong."

"What do you mean?"

Lennox jumped in. "Your mother and I pushed you into getting this degree even though it might not have been your choice."

"I wanted it," Sienna said. "Maybe not as much as you did, but I did." With a start, Sienna realized how true those words were. She did feel a great sense of accomplishment, and she should be celebrating.

Before she could second-guess her decision, Sienna blurted out, "I'm going to throw myself a big to-do to celebrate." She shimmied. "It will be black tie and…" She snapped her fingers as her enthusiasm grew. "Maybe I'll do a theme."

Her father relaxed. "See, I told you we had nothing to worry about," Lennox said to her mom. "Sienna's a fighter. She doesn't stay down for long."

Sienna nodded and forced a smile.

Daphne cleared her throat. "Do you plan on inviting Joel to your party?"

"Leave it alone, Daphne." Lennox's voice held a warning.

Her bravado slipped. Sienna said softly, "I don't think he'll want to come."

Daphne came to sit by her side. "You two seemed so well-suited." She placed an arm around Sienna's shoulder. "I'm a performer. I know all about pushing through the pain when heartache is like a ringing in your ear." She touched her chest with her free hand. "It hurts me to see you hurting. If we hadn't pushed for education over love, maybe you wouldn't be sitting here, trying to hide the fact that you were probably crying before we arrived."

Her mother truly saw her. Saw past the bluff and knew the truth. Tears pooled in her eyes. Sienna nodded. "I'm in love with him."

"I knew it. That's why you argue with him so much. I was like that with your father."

Her mouth dropped. "What? I never see you two argue."

"Correct." Daphne nodded. "You never saw. Doesn't mean we never did—or that we still don't."

Her father pursed his lips, refusing to look Sienna's way. "I don't want our daughter fighting like we did."

"She's as fiery as I am." Her mother's voice was light. Daphne went over to kiss Lennox on the cheek.

Sienna dabbed at her eyes, feeling as if she were in a dream. Then a realization occurred: this conversation was the result of answered prayer. All she could do was whisper a heartfelt thanks to God for how He had healed and was healing her past relationships.

Maybe He was doing that to prepare her for something bigger. Something amazing, like a life-lasting love with Joel. All she had to do was accept. Sienna smiled. If God meant this for her, Joel didn't have a choice either.

"Are you going to call that man or should I?" Daphne asked.

"I've got it, Mom." Sienna stood, rushed into her room to toss some clothes into her carry-on before returning to the living room. "Make yourselves at home. I'll be back tomorrow."

Her father's brows rose to his hairline. "'Tomorrow'?"

"Well, maybe a couple of days. It all depends. I have a plane to catch." Sienna grabbed her purse and strode toward the door. "I'm going to Louisiana, and I'm coming back with my man."

He could live here.

Joel sat in the two-seater swing in the huge backyard of his brother's house, enjoying the tranquility of holding Micah in his arms and having no deadlines. The backyard was a toddler's dream. There was a playground, a junior shed and a trampoline. Greg had installed the equipment and new grass when he learned he was going to have a child. Joel couldn't wait to see Micah playing with all this stuff.

It was a warm, sunny day, and the skyline was crystal clear. Joel sighed. He couldn't ask for anything more.

Well, he could. But that hadn't worked out.

However, seeing his nephew's trusting face and being close to him was doing wonders for Joel's heart. He was going to bestow all the love he had to give on Micah. Micah wouldn't turn him down or leave him out in the rain.

Nope.

Greg and Tessa had gone out to dinner at Joel's request. The new parents were worn out and needed time together alone. He had taken the liberty of making a reservation for them at a nearby restaurant, and they had been so grateful, knowing Joel was more than capable of caring for their son.

"It's just you and me, bud." Joel tucked his legs under the swing and pushed off, liking the squeaky sound. He hadn't told his brother yet, but Joel had started looking into editorial positions in Shreveport and the nearby town of Bossier City. There were a few promising prospects and he had even received a callback.

There was only one person stopping him.

Sienna. Despite everything, the thought of not seeing her twisted up his insides like a mangled wire. He dug into his pants pocket for the ring he had purchased. Joel wasn't sure why he kept it in his pocket, but he looked at it every day. It was a symbol of his defeat when it came to love and a reminder not to try it again. A flashback of his humiliating pleas in the rain made him cringe. That hadn't been one of his best moments, but he didn't regret putting himself out there. With a sigh, he returned the ring to his pocket.

After leaving her apartment, Joel had driven over to see Skip to tender his resignation. Then he had ventured to the church to see August, who had done his best to cheer Joel and pray for him. Joel had hibernated at home before impulsively returning to Shreveport.

That had been a great idea. There was nothing like peace.

A voice boomed behind him, shattering the calm. "You have a lot of nerve coming down here without me."

Joel clutched Micah and spun around to face the woman who filled his thoughts more often than he would ever admit. She had her hands on her hips and looked like a glorious Amazon warrior, ready to avenge. It thrilled and scared him at the same time. "Sienna?"

"That's *Dr.* King to you." She stomped toward him, her fancy sandals dipping into the earth.

"Congratulations… Wh-what are you doing here?" If he wasn't holding Micah, he would have pinched himself to make sure he hadn't fallen asleep.

She whispered with fury. "What do you think?" her eyes fiery, "I came to get you." Her face softened. "And to see my favorite person."

"You came to get me?" Hope flared in his chest. Joy at being in her presence made his stomach flutter. Micah squirmed but settled.

"I told you not to keep holding that baby once he's sleeping." She pointed to the door. "Let's get inside from this heat."

He squinted. Sienna was behaving as if she hadn't ignored him the last time she saw him. Memories of the way she had misjudged him regarding her mother's article kindled Joel's anger. He opened the sliding door and gestured for her to enter before stepping inside. He would put Micah down to finish his nap, grab the baby monitor and then they were going to thrash this out.

Joel joined Sienna, who sat on the edge of the brown leather sectional. The space was decorated in warm browns and oranges, and boasted a huge television and a large fireplace.

"You've got a lot of nerve barging in here after how you treated me," he spat out once he was back in the living room.

"Love gives me the nerve." She lifted her chin, not the least bit apologetic. "I love you."

"You love me?" he snarled. "You have a funny way of showing it. Kicking me to the curb the way you did." At the same time, his heart began to sing, *She loves me! She loves me!* He clamped his lips tight to keep the stupid smile at bay.

She stood and took his hand in hers. "I'm sorry. I do love you." This time she sounded penitent. "Please tell me it's not too late… Although, if it is too late, then I'd question if you really loved me in the first place. Because if it is genuine love, then that means it wouldn't wither like grass in the heat."

Joel slapped his forehead. "Wow. You are exasperating." And perfect for him.

She quirked her lips and gave him a tender look. "Tell me something I don't know." She touched his face tenderly.

Joel dropped to one knee in front of her and pulled out the ring. "Dr. Sienna King, I–"

"Wait. You conveniently have an engagement ring in your pocket?" Her voice held suspicion.

He sighed. As usual, Sienna was being difficult. "What does it matter? I bought it a couple weeks ago, and I've been carrying it around ever since."

"Did you have it that day outside my apartment?"

All he could do was nod. At that, Sienna buried her face in her hands and sobbed. Joel stood and wrapped his arms around her.

"I'm sorry," she wailed. "I should have opened the door."

"Yes, you should have, but you're here now. I'm glad you realize you can't do without me."

As he had expected and intended, she stiffened. Lifting her tear-streaked face, she jabbed his chest. "Don't get it twisted. I can do without you. I just choose not to."

He smiled and ran his hands through her strands. "I choose you too. For life. I love you, and I want to fight with you and love on you every day for the rest of my life. Will you marry me?"

"Do you think I would be here if I wasn't planning on it?" She sniffled and held out her hand. "I hope you got the right size."

Oh, his Sienna. The days ahead would never be dull. Of that, he was sure. With a chuckle, Joel slipped the ring on her finger. Her sparkling diamond was no match for the radiance she brought to his heart.

For once, she was speechless. "It's so beautiful. You did good."

Joel gazed at her beautiful face and whispered, "Yes. Yes, I truly did."

Epilogue

"It's pouring out there, and I have a pimple." Sienna stood by the sliding doors of her hotel room in Ocho Rios, Jamaica, watching the torrential downpour and the dark clouds. Her lips quivered. Today should be one of the best days of her life. Her wedding day. Her braids had been styled in a topknot threaded with faux pearls and her wedding dress was a blend of lace and chiffon that had melted her heart when she had tried it on. But if the weather was any indication, her life with Joel would be anything but blue skies.

"I'm not the least bit surprised," Jade said, smoothing her ankle length purple gown. "And you shouldn't be either."

Sienna lifted a brow. "What do you mean?"

"Nothing about you and Joel has been conventional. So, why should the weather on the most important day of your lives be boring?" Jade pointed towards the turbulence. Thunder clapped. "No, my friend, this is a day you'll remember."

Pointing to her cheek, her nails the same shade of

purple as Jade's dress, Sienna chuckled, "So, is that why I have a ginormous pimple on my face?"

Jade lifted her hands. "For that, I have no words. I told you to stop eating the chocolate candies and switch to ice chips."

"It's my nerves. It's not every day a girl pledges to spend eternity with the man of her dreams."

"If Kelsey was here, she would know what to say."

"Yeah, well, unlike me Kelsey had the good sense not to travel to the Caribbean during hurricane season."

"You know the only reason she isn't here is because the twins got sick."

Jade crossed her eyes "Potato. Po*tah*to."

Sienna giggled. "Quit trying to make me laugh."

Wagging a finger, Jade said, "There'll be no sad tears on your wedding day. Only happy ones."

The wind howled and the rain beat against the glass of the door. Sienna thought of the makeshift altar on the beach that was most likely destroyed. She pictured the purple and white flowers for the garland shredded on the sand and groaned. The wedding planner had told her not to worry, that everything would be set up in the chapel, but Sienna's stomach knotted.

There was a rap on the door. Jade hurried to see who was on the other side.

Seconds later, Sienna saw her mother's smiling face. Daphne was dressed in a champagne off-the-shoulder gown with a matching clutch under her arm. Her hair framed her cheeks and her skin glowed. Daphne was still in remission and in good health. Sienna whispered a word of thanksgiving.

"You look stunning," Daphne said, her eyes glowing.

"I hope Joel thinks so when he sees this huge zit on my face."

"That man loves you. He's not worried about something that will clear up in a matter of days. He's with you for a lifetime."

Sienna exhaled. "You sound so sure. So…calm."

Daphne patted her purse. "Of course. It also helps that Jade told me to bring my special concealer."

At that Sienna started laughing. Soon, her mother and Jade joined in and her heart lightened. Though it was storming on the outside, she felt nothing but joy on the inside. Joy for the man who made her smile, who challenged her and who was her equal. And that's what she would focus on when she walked down the aisle.

Joel stood under the awning in the chapel hoping no one would see him shaking. Not from fear but from anticipation. Today he was marrying the woman he couldn't wait to make his.

The past few months had been torturous and wonderful at the same time. He couldn't wait to hold Sienna in his arms and show her off. Sienna didn't know it but he had a special guest waiting to see her in the first row. He waved at Micah, bouncing on his mother's lap.

Greg stood next to him. He had asked Joel at least three times if he was sure and if he needed an escape route, until Joel had jabbed him in the chest, to quit playing. Since getting to know his brother over the past year, Joel had learned Greg was quite the tease.

He pulled on the bow tie of his traditional tuxedo before raking a hand through his curls. He had grown his hair at Sienna's request.

Seeing the organist scuttle down the aisle and take her seat at the organ, Joel glanced at his watch and smiled. His Sienna would be right on time.

When the melody to *Fools Rush In* began to play exactly two minutes later, Joel watched as Jade strutted down the aisle, holding a bouquet of purple and white.

Then when the wedding processional began, he held his breath until he saw his first glimpse of Sienna. When she rounded the corner, with her father next to her, Joel gasped. Her dress enhanced her best features and the only jewelry she wore was her engagement ring. All he could think as she came toward him was, she was his. And, she was here. As she had told him many times during their year of premarital counseling, she had no intentions of going anywhere.

Her exact words were, he was stuck with her. Words he had needed to hear.

His eyes misted.

Soon, she was standing next to him. He gestured toward Micah, watching her face brighten. She went to kiss Micah on the cheek and returned to his side.

Then the officiant began with some corny wedding humor, while Joel struggled to remain patient. He was ready to skip everything and kiss his bride.

Sienna pointed to her face and whispered under her breath, "I got a pimple."

"So do I but I prefer to call it a love bump." He tapped his chin before squeezing her hand. "You're still gorgeous."

Hearing a loud clearing of the throat, both Sienna and Joel focused on the man standing before them. "If you two are ready, Joel and Sienna will address each other before the exchanging of the vows."

Outside the thunder boomed but Joel only had eyes for the woman who now faced him.

"Joel, we spent a couple decades fighting. Literally. But there is no fighting how I feel about you. Moments before walking down the aisle, I was worried about the weather. I was worried about the hotel losing power. But the one thing I wasn't worried about was marrying you."

She touched his cheek. "I knew when it came to you, I was making the best decision of my life. I can't wait for us to start a family and to begin the rest of our lives together. I promise to be the best wife that I can be for you. I will pray for you. I will be by your side. I will treasure our love, always."

After a loud sniffle, Joel wiped his cheeks with the back of his hand and straightened.

"Sienna, I was prepared to live alone, remain single forever. But God had other plans." His voice cracked. "He sent me the most infuriating, determined woman… perfect for me in every way." Joel couldn't finish all he planned to say. All he could do was enfold Sienna in his arms.

Fortunately, the minister rescued him by leading Joel and Sienna in their traditional vows. Then it was time for the kiss. He could hear his brother whooping next to him.

She looked at him, her eyes full of love. "I love you, Mr. Armstrong."

"I love you, too, Sienna."

She tapped his nose. "That's Mrs. Armstrong to you."

"Mrs. Armstrong," he breathed out, before pressing his lips to hers. The crowd cheered.

Pulling away from him, Sienna said, “Joel, we’ve got guests waiting. You can’t kiss me forever.”

With a grin, he said, “Challenge accepted,” before lowering his head to hers.

* * * * *

Dear Reader,

I fell in love with Sienna and Joel while writing The Adoption Surprise. Their chemistry cracked me up from the start, and though they were secondary characters, they were standouts. I knew these feisty characters would need a special circumstance to bring them together, because, boy, do they love to argue! And caring for a newborn was the perfect situation.

Sienna and Joel were two independent, self-sufficient people who had to put their pride aside and work together to make sure Micah was okay. It was great seeing their friendship develop over shared experiences and a common goal into something deeper.

I really got a kick out of writing this enemies-to-love story, and I hope you enjoyed watching these characters fall in love as much as I did. I would love to hear your thoughts. Please connect with me on Facebook or join my newsletter at www.zoeymariejackson.com.

Thanks,
Zoey Marie

COMING NEXT MONTH FROM
Love Inspired

HIS FORGOTTEN AMISH LOVE
by Rebecca Kertz

Two years ago, David Troyer asked to court Fannie Miller...then disappeared without a trace. Suddenly he's back with no memory of her, and she's tasked with catering his family reunion. Where has he been and why has he forgotten her? Will her heart be broken all over again?

THE AMISH SPINSTER'S DILEMMA
by Jocelyn McClay

When a mysterious *Englisch* granddaughter is dropped into widower Thomas Reihl's life, he turns to neighbor Emma Beiler for help. The lonely spinster bonds with the young girl and helps Thomas teach her their Amish ways. Can they both convince Thomas that he needs to start living—and loving—again?

A FRIEND TO TRUST
K-9 Companions • by Lee Tobin McClain

Working at a summer camp isn't easy for Pastor Nate Fisher. Especially since he's sharing the director job with standoffish Hayley Harris. But when Nate learns a secret about one of their campers that affects Hayley, he'll have to decide if their growing connection can withstand the truth.

THE COWBOY'S LITTLE SECRET
Wyoming Ranchers • by Jill Kemerer

Struggling cattle rancher Austin Watkins can't believe his son's nanny is quitting. Cassie Berber wants to pursue her dreams in the big city—even though she cares for the infant and his dad. Can Austin convince her to stay and build a home with them in Wyoming?

LOVING THE RANCHER'S CHILDREN
Hope Crossing • by Mindy Obenhaus

Widower Jake Walker needs a nanny for his kids. But with limited options in their small town, he turns to former friend Alli Krenek. Alli doesn't want anything to do with the single dad, but when she finds herself falling for his children, she'll try to overcome their past and see what the future holds...

HIS SWEET SURPRISE
by Angie Dicken

Returning to his family's orchard, Lance Hudson is seeking a fresh start. He never expects to be working alongside his first love, single mom Piper Gray. When Piper reveals she's the mother of a child he never knew about, Lance must decide if he'll step up and be the man she needs.

LOOK FOR THESE AND OTHER LOVE INSPIRED BOOKS WHEREVER BOOKS ARE SOLD, INCLUDING MOST BOOKSTORES, SUPERMARKETS, DISCOUNT STORES AND DRUGSTORES.

LICNM0423